NOVE[illegible] COCAIN[illegible]

Novel with Cocaine

M. Ageyev

Translated by Michael Henry Heim

NORTHWESTERN UNIVERSITY PRESS
EVANSTON, ILLINOIS

Northwestern University Press
625 Colfax Street
Evanston, Illinois 60208-4210

First European Classics printing 1998

ISBN 0-8101-1709-6

Library of Congress Cataloging-in-Publication Data

Agïeev, M.
[Roman s kokainom. English]
Novel with cocaine / M. Ageyev ; translated by Michael Henry Heim.
p. cm. — (European classics)
ISBN 0-8101-1709-6 (alk. paper)
I. Heim, Michael Henry. II. Title. III. Series: European classics (Evanston, Ill.)
PG3476.A3164R613 1998
891.73'44—dc21 98-22090
CIP

The paper used in this publication meets the minimum requirements of the American National Standard for Information Sciences—Permanence of Paper for Printed Library Materials, ANSI Z39.48-1984.

TRANSLATOR'S INTRODUCTION

Novel with Cocaine is a story of adolescent addiction. The extremes of ecstasy and despair that Vadim, the Russian hero, passes through when under the influence of cocaine are in fact heightened projections of the conflicts he sees around him as he enters the adult world. Only after relating formative experiences at school and with women does he turn to the rites of initiation (the loss of "nasal virginity," as one of the characters puts it) and the everyday humiliation of the habit. If the hyper-conscious, hyper-sensitive Vadim is categorical in his condemnation of the adult world—the novel takes place in Moscow immediately before and after the 1917 Revolution—he is positively scathing in his judgments of himself.

A work as searingly personal and confessional as *Novel with Cocaine* might be expected to contain a core of autobiographical material. Whether it does or not we cannot say for sure: we know next to nothing about M. Ageyev; in fact, since "M. Ageyev" is a pseudonym, we do not even know his name. All we do know is that in the early thirties a Paris-based Russian émigré journal, *Numbers,* received an unsolicited manuscript from Istanbul, a manuscript entitled *Story with Cocaine.* Following the *succès de scandale* of its journal publication, it appeared as a book under the title *Novel with Cocaine* (a pun of sorts in Russian, since *roman,* the Russian word for "novel," may also be construed as "romance"), then disappeared, seemingly forever.

Now, about fifty years later, it has resurfaced. One of the work's early admirers (and, we are told, a close friend or relative of the author) came upon it in a second-hand bookshop in Paris and immediately set about translating it into French. At the same time she tried to uncover as much information as she could about the author. Rumor and speculation aside, all that has come to light is this: "Ageyev," a Russian émigré living in Istanbul, wished to move to Paris and establish his reputation as a writer there. Encouraged by the reception of *Novel with Cocaine,* he sent first a short story, then his passport to a friend in Paris. The short story was published, the passport lost. Recent attempts to locate him by means of notices in the French and Turkish press have proved fruitless. Neither the friend nor anyone else has ever heard from him again.

Assuming Ageyev to be the age of his hero, we may wish to imagine him a venerable octogenarian living out his life in seclusion. The most probable of the speculations about his fate, however, is that he returned to the Soviet Union, and any émigré returning at the time of Stalin's purges faced almost certain arrest and deportation to the death camps. The novel itself provides clear enough evidence of Ageyev's disdain for the pre-Revolutionary, *belle epoque* society in which the hero lived—the chasm between rich and poor and the multilevel exploitation that chasm caused—but it also points to the danger inherent in any system claiming to regulate mankind, regulate it totally, even if "for its own good." Ageyev demonstrates his ambiguity towards the new regime in the novel's beautifully ambiguous, O. Henry-like ending. Surely his is the first Russian novel to span the period between 1916 and 1919 yet never once mention the Revolution. And his reticence notwithstanding, the few post-Revolutionary pages tell us more about what happened in those years than whole chapters of detailed accounts.

Not that *Novel with Cocaine* is primarily political in content or intent. Not in the least. In France, where the recent translation of the work was extremely well received, critics repeatedly compared Ageyev to Proust; they pointed to his effective use of emotional memory and association and to the long, sinuous patterns of his sentences. We might also invoke the De Quincey of *Confessions of an English Opium Eater,* for the honesty with which he transcribes his terrifying hallucinations; and the Salinger of *The Catcher in the Rye,* for the honesty with which he characterizes the adolescent dilemma. Like Holden Caulfield, Ageyev's Vadim consciously wants nothing more than to grow up; yet, again like Holden, he is unconsciously frightened to death of the prospect. At first, Vadim seems to plow straight on where Holden temporizes, but the moment cocaine comes his way, he embraces the passivity it offers. For cocaine allows him to believe he has grown up—believe that his wildest dreams of success have come true—without the slightest effort on his part.

Of course, we must not overlook the Russian tradition. Ageyev's perception of his hero, his view of character psychology in general, owes most to Dostoevsky. Vadim continues the long line of Dostoevskian humiliated and self-humiliating heroes; he exemplifies, in a sense, the Dostoevskian double. But Vadim is a "self-conscious" double: he has the advantage of having read Dostoevsky and ruminated long and hard on the duality of his own nature and the nature of mankind.

If, in the end, Vadim's ruminations reveal him to be not so much a mature thinker as a bright and highly disturbed adolescent, they merely remind us that *Novel with Cocaine* is not so much a philosophical as a psychological novel. For its insight into the psychology of adolescence and the psychology of cocaine dependence, for its period atmosphere and period style, and above all for its honesty, we must be grateful for the reappearance of a work that seems destined to remain a mystery.

MICHAEL HENRY HEIM

NOVEL WITH COCAINE

SCHOOL

Burkewitz refuses.

1

Early one morning I, Vadim Maslennikov, set off for school (I was going on seventeen at the time) having forgotten the envelope with the first-semester fees Mother had left for me in the dining room the day before. I did not think of it until I was in the tram watching the gathering speed turn boulevard fences and acacias from flashing spikes to a continuous flow and feeling the burden on my shoulders press me harder and harder against a nickel grip. Nor was I in the least upset by my forgetfulness. I could hand in the money the next day, and there was no one at home to make off with it: the only other person in the flat besides Mother and me was my old nanny, who had been in our service for more than twenty-five years and whose only weakness (and, possibly, only passion) was to maintain a constant whisper, as resonant as the crack of sunflower seeds, in which, for want of company, she would carry on endless conversations and even arguments with herself, now and then interrupting them with loud, stentorian exclamations such as "Why, of course!" or "I should say so!" or "Don't count on it!"

By the time I arrived at school I had completely forgotten about the envelope. As it happened—and it did not happen often—I had failed to do my lessons for the day and was forced to prepare them partly during the breaks and partly during the classes themselves, while the teacher lectured, and the intense state of concentration that makes everything so easy to learn (though just as easy to forget the next day) further cleared my mind of extraneous matters. Not until the main break began—when, because the weather, though cold, was dry and sunny, we were allowed into the courtyard and on the way out I saw Mother standing on the lower landing of the staircase—not until then did I recall the envelope and realize that she had been unable to bear the thought of its remaining behind and had brought it herself. She stood alone, off to the side, in her fur coat full of bald patches and her ludicrous bonnet fringed with strands of gray hair (she was fifty-seven at the time), peering into the streaming throng with obvious trepidation, which only heightened her pitiful appearance. Somc of the students turned to look at her; they laughed and made remarks. As I came closer, I tried to hide and slip by unnoticed, but she soon spotted me, and lighting up with a smile that, warm as it was, had more humility about it than cheer, she called out my name. Embarrassed as I was to be seen in her presence by my fellow students, I went over to her.

"Vadichka, darling," she said in a dull, old woman's voice, holding out the envelope in her yellow hand and touching a button of my overcoat apprehensively as if it might burn her. "You forgot the money, my boy, and I thought you'd be worried. Here it is, I've brought it to you."

So saying, she looked up at me as if begging for alms. I, however, enraged by the shame she had inflicted on me, whispered spitefully that this was no place for mawkish sentiments, that since she couldn't wait to bring the money she should go and pay it herself. She stood there listening mutely, her tender eyes meekly, painfully lowered. There was nothing for me to do but race down the already empty stairs. And if after pulling open the door, so heavy it sucked the air in with a noisy swish, I turned and looked back at her, I did so not at all out of pity but for fear she would choose so inappropriate a place to burst into tears. There she was, sadly craning her grotesque head forward to follow my every move. As soon as she saw me look in her direction, she waved the hand with the envelope at me the way friends wave good-bye at the station—a youthful, sprightly gesture that only emphasized how pitifully tattered and worn she was.

Outside in the courtyard a few of my classmates came up to me. Who was that clown in a petticoat I'd been talking to? they wanted to know. I laughed and said she was an impoverished governess who had come to me with some letters of recommendation; if they liked I could arrange an introduction: they could easily have their way with the likes of her.

No sooner had I said it than I realized, not so much from the words themselves as from the guffaws they provoked, that this time even I had gone too far and that I should have held my tongue. And when, having made the payment, Mother came out looking straight ahead and, hunched over as if to make herself even smaller, hurried as fast as her crooked, run-down heels would take her across the asphalt path to the gate, I felt my heart going painfully out to her.

The pain, which so stung me at first, did not last: it had all but disappeared by the time I returned home from school, though as I walked through the entrance hall—along the narrow, smelly passage of our wretched little flat and into my room—I felt enough of a residue to remind me of what it had felt like an hour before; and by the time I was sitting at table and watching Mother serve the soup, I realized I had not only completely overcome it, but found it difficult to imagine how I could have been bothered by it in the first place.

Yet no sooner did I feel relief than I was plagued by a rush of vicious thoughts: that the old crone ought to have realized she would put me to shame wearing those rags of hers, that she had no business coming to the school with the envelope, that she had forced me to lie and therefore deprived me of the opportunity to invite my friends home. I watched her eating her soup, lifting the spoon with a trembling hand and spilling part of it back into the bowl; I watched her yellow cheeks, her nose, carrot red from the heat of the soup, watched her, after each swallow, lick the fat from her lips with a tongue coated white—and hated her with a passion. Feeling my gaze on her, she looked back at me, tenderly as always, with her faded brown eyes, then put down her spoon, and presumably compelled by having looked at me to say something, she asked, "Do you like the soup?"

She said it with a child-like intonation, cocking her gray head as if begging for approval.

"Wike the thoup," I responded, neither approvingly nor disapprovingly, mocking her. I said it with a disgusting grimace, too, as though I had just had an attack of nausea, and our eyes—mine cold and hateful, hers warm and inward-looking—met and merged.

We remained thus for a long time, and I could clearly see the gleam in her eyes fade and turn to puzzlement, then pain, but the more I felt victorious the less I was able to feel and comprehend my hatred for a person so vulnerable and full of love, the hatred that had earned me my victory. That must be why I gave in, lowered my eyes first, and picked up my spoon to resume eating. But when, inwardly composed and wishing to say something trivial, I again raised my head, I surprised myself by leaping up out of my chair instead.

She rested the hand with the spoon on the tablecloth and, leaning her elbow on the table, propped her head in the other hand. Her thin lips, stretching cheekwards, twisted her face out of shape, and from the brown sockets of her closed eyes through the fans of her wrinkles the tears began to flow. Moved by the defenselessness of an aging yellow head and meek yet bitter grief, the hopelessness of a repugnant, totally useless old age, but still looking sidelong at her and using a rough voice that could only have sounded suspicious, I said, "There, there, don't cry . . . Come now, wipe your tears . . . There's nothing to cry about, is there?" and was just about to add a "Mother, dear" and perhaps even go up and kiss her when Nanny, balancing on one of her felt-booted legs and kicking the door open with the other, came in from the passage with the main course.

Suddenly—I have no idea for what purpose or whose sake—I came down with my fist in the soup plate, and convinced once and for all of the legitimacy of my position by the pain in my hand and by my soup-stained trousers, a feeling dimly reinforced by Nanny's terrible fright, I let out a menacing oath and stalked off to my room.

A short time later Mother put on her coat and hat and went out. She did not return until evening. I heard her footsteps move directly from the entrance hall down the passage to my door. She knocked and asked, "May I come in?" and I rushed over to my desk, threw open a book, and sitting down, my back to the door, responded with a bored, "Yes, do."

She walked across the room irresolutely, coming up to me from the side, and while I, supposedly deep in my books, looked on surreptitiously, she slipped her hand inside her fur coat and ludicrous black bonnet and came out with two five-ruble bills, discreetly crumpled as if to take up as little space as possible, and laid them on my desk. Then, running her arthritic hand through my hair, she said softly, "You will forgive me, my son? You're a good boy. I know you are." And lost in thought, running her hand through my hair again, she seemed on the point of saying something more. In the end, however, she left on tiptoe without a word, shutting the door behind her.

2

Not long thereafter I fell ill. My initial fright, which was considerable, quickly dissipated in the face of the matter-of-fact, cheery manner of the doctor I had chosen at random from the venereologists who took up nearly an entire page in the newspaper. Examining me, he opened his eyes wide with respect and astonishment, much as our literature professor was wont to do when receiving a good answer from a bad student. Then, patting me on the back, he assured me (not in a consolatory tone, which would have spoiled the mood, but with the calm conviction of his curative powers), "Don't worry, my boy. We'll have you all patched up in a month."

After washing his hands, writing out the necessary prescriptions, and telling me how to follow them (all the while ignoring the ruble piece I had awkwardly sent careering across his glass-topped desk with a clink that grew into a proper drumroll as it came to rest), the doctor gave his nose a hearty scratch and sent me off on a note of somber concern which ill became him, that is, with the warning that the speed of my recovery, if not the recovery itself, depended entirely on the regularity of my visits and I would do well to see him daily.

Before the week was out I realized that daily sessions were far from essential and that the doctor was merely using them as a way to increase the frequency of my ruble's clink in his office. I continued to keep my appointments nevertheless. I kept them purely because I enjoyed them. There was something about the stubby, roly-poly little man, something about his unctuous bass voice, that made him sound as if he had just polished off a tasty morsel, about the folds in his blubbery neck that resembled a pile of bicycle tires, about his jolly, crafty eyes, and about his overall attitude towards me—something clownishly boastful yet adulatory, something that I could not quite put my finger on but that was pleasantly flattering. He was the first grown man—the first adult, in other words—who saw me and understood me the way I wanted to appear. And when I went for my daily appointment, I felt I was going to see a friend rather than a doctor, so much so that in the beginning, at least, I could hardly wait for the appointed hour to come, and dressed for it as for a ball in my new jacket and trousers and in my black patent-leather pumps.

It was during those days, when, trying to establish myself as an erotic *Wunderkind*, I told my classmates about the illness I had contracted (I said it had been cured when in fact it had only just begun) and hadn't the slightest doubt that I would thereby gain stature in their eyes—it was in those days that I committed a terrible act, an act resulting in the mutilation of a human life and perhaps even in death.

One evening about a fortnight after my first visit to the doctor, at a time when the external symptoms had begun to abate though I knew perfectly well I was still afflicted, I stepped out to take a walk or go to the pictures. It was that splendid time of year that is mid-November. The first downy snowflakes fell leisurely on Moscow like shards of marble in deep-blue water. The rooftops and flowerbeds along the boulevards swelled up into light-blue sails. There was no clicking of horseshoes, no scraping of wheels; the tram bells' unsettling, Spring-like message rang out clearly over the hushed city.

Walking along the street, I happened to catch up with a girl walking ahead of me—not because I meant to, simply because I was moving at a faster pace. But just as I was about to pass her, I sank into a snowbank and she looked back. Our eyes met, and smiled. On that most passionate of Moscow nights, the night of the first snowfall, when cheeks are tinged cranberry red and the wires are like taut gray cables, on such a night, where can one find the strength—or solemnity—to part in silence, never to meet again?

I asked her what her name was and where she was going. Her name was Zinochka and she was going "nowhere in particular," she was "just out for a stroll." At the corner we came upon a worthy steed draped in a white horsecloth and hitched to a sleigh of the type that rises high off the ground like a goblet. I suggested we go for a spin, and Zinochka—her eyes flashing, her lips pursed like a button—nodded yes over and over like a child. The driver was stuffed into the question-mark front of the sleigh with his side to us, but when we walked by he came to life and, fixing us with his eyes as if aiming at a moving target, fired a hoarse "How's about a ride, your Honor?" in our direction. Then, seeing he had hit his mark and the time had come to bag it, he climbed down from the sleigh—footless, green, and overbearingly majestic, wearing white gloves the size of a child's head and a sawed-off Onegin-like top hat complete with buckle—lumbered up to us, and said, "Give me the word, your Honor, and I'll give you a run for your money."

Then the torture began. He asked ten rubles to take us out to Petrovsky Park and back. "Your Honor" had only five rubles fifty in his pocket, yet I was perfectly ready to jump aboard, certain as I was at that age that yielding to the most obvious fraud would leave less of a stain on my honor than sinking to bargain with a driver in the presence of a lady. Luckily, Zinochka came to my rescue. With indignation welling in her eyes, she announced in no uncertain terms that ten rubles was an outrageous price and I was not to give him any more than three. As she talked, she pulled me away by the arm and I half trailed along, putting up just enough resistance to transfer the stigma of the situation from myself to her: to make it seem that, while I of course was willing to pay whatever he asked, I had no say in the matter.

After we had gone about twenty steps, Zinochka looked back over my shoulder with the caution of a thief and, seeing the horsecloth sliding down the horse's back, sidled up to me on tiptoe and whispered in my ear, all but squealing from excitement, "He's changed his mind. He's changed his mind." Then she clapped her hands noiselessly a few times. "He's going to take us," she went on. "See how clever I am?" She kept trying to look me in the eye. "See? See?"

That "See? See?" was very sweet to my ears. It meant that I was an elegant rake, rich and profligate, and she a poor, destitute little girl intent on holding down my expenses—not because they might ruin me, no, but because the narrow horizons of poverty prevented her from even conceiving such extravagance.

At the next crossroads the driver caught up and passed us, and skillfully holding back his steed by snapping the reins first to the right, then to the left, like a rudder, he lay back into the sleigh and unhooked the traveling rug. I helped Zinochka up and, fighting the impulse to rush, walked deliberately round to the other side, where I too mounted the high, narrow seat. Then I slipped the stiff velvet loop into its metal pin, put my arm around Zinochka, and, giving the visor of my cap a good, strong tug, as if about to start a fight, I spit out an arrogant, "Ready."

The horse lurched forward with a lazy smack of the lips, and as the sleigh started inching along I felt myself trembling with rage at the driver's mockery. But when after two turns we came out on Tverskaya-Yamskaya, he suddenly gathered the reins and cried out "Ey-yep!"—with the sharp, steely *e* rising stridently to meet the soft yet effective buffer of the *p*. Suddenly the sleigh gave a violent lurch, and we were first thrown back, knees in the air, then immediately forward, our faces in the driver's padded back. Now the entire street rushed at us, thongs of wet snow lashing our cheeks and eyes, and trams raced past calling out to us, and we answered—first with another "*Ey-yep!*" but shorter, more clipped, whip-like, then with the joyfully malicious bleat of "*Baloo-oo-ee!*"—and the black flashes of sleighs from the opposite direction, the terrifying prospect of a shaft in the face, the *chok, chok, chok* of slush hurled by the horse's shoes against the sleigh's metal front, the whole sleigh vibrating, our hearts vibrating . . .

"Oh, how good it feels!" the childish voice next to me kept whispering in the wet, stinging rain. "Oh, how marvelous! How marvelous!"

I felt "marvelous" as well, yet I was also doing everything I could to resist, to counteract the excitement raging within me.

When we swept past the Yar and into sight of the tram station tower and the boarded-up sweets stand near the entrance to the park, the driver leaned back almost on top of us and pulled in the horse, intoning a series of short *prr*'s in a gentle, woman's voice. We entered the park at a walk just as the snow stopped falling, though we could still see it flying listlessly round the single yellow streetlamp, like down from a quilt being shaken. In the black air beyond the streetlamp there was a wooden fist—with protruding index finger, cuff, and the beginnings of a sleeve—nailed crookedly to a tree. Along the finger walked a raven, scattering snow.

I asked Zinochka whether she felt cold. "I feel marvelous," she answered. "It is marvelous, isn't it? Here, take my hands and warm them up." I disengaged my arm from around her waist; it was beginning to ache in any case. The water from my cap had started dripping behind my collar, both our faces were sopping wet, and the cold had so constricted our chins and cheeks that we were forced to speak without moving our mouths; moreover, our eyebrows and lashes had frozen together into icicles, the traveling rug and the front, shoulders, and sleeves of our coats were covered with a crisp layer of frost, Zinochka's cheeks looked pasted over with bright red apple peels, and the steam disgorged by all of us, including the horse, appeared to rise out of boiling cauldrons.

The deserted road running round the park was all white and blue, and in its white and blue naphthalene shimmer, its motionless, chamber-like quiet, I suddenly descried my misery. I remembered that in several minutes I would be back in town—dismissing the sleigh, going home, fiddling with my odious disease, and getting up the next morning in the dark. Suddenly I no longer felt so marvelous.

It was an odd thing about my life: whenever I was happy, I would think my happiness could not last; as soon as I thought that, it would indeed go up in smoke. Not because the external conditions creating it had ceased to exist, but because I was conscious that in due course those external conditions *would* cease to exist, inevitably. Yes, as soon as that consciousness made itself felt, I lost all feeling of happiness, and the external conditions, which still existed, merely grated on me. By the time we had circled the park and come out on the main road, I had only one desire: to get back to town as fast as possible, pay off the driver, and leave the sleigh.

The trip back was cold and boring, but when we reached the Monastery of the Passion and the driver turned to ask whether he should keep going and if so in what direction, I glanced questioningly at Zinochka and suddenly felt my heart stopping in the usual, sensual way. For she was looking at my lips, not my eyes, looking with a dull, savage expression I understood immediately. Leaning forward on my knees, which were quivering with delight, I told the driver to take us to Vinogradov's.

It would be absolutely wrong to assume that

during the few minutes it took to drive to the *maison de rendez-vous* I was unconcerned about passing on my illness to Zinochka. Pressing her against me, I thought of nothing else; but my thoughts centered not so much on the responsibility I might incur as on the trouble others might cause me. And as is so often the case in these matters, fear of discovery did not in the least deter me from the act; it simply led me to go about it in such a way that no one would know who had perpetrated it.

The sleigh stopped in front of a reddish building with caulked windows, and I asked the driver to pull into the courtyard. To pass through the gateway, we had to back up to the boulevard fence, and as we were going forward again we cut into the asphalt with a screech, the sleigh swerving diagonally across the walkway. During the several seconds it took the horse to gather its strength for the lunge that would carry us into the courtyard, the passersby, forced to walk round the sleigh, stared at us with curiosity. Two of them even stopped, a circumstance not lost on Zinochka. She immediately seemed more aloof: reserved, wounded, worried.

While Zinochka climbed down from the sleigh and hurried off into a dark corner, I tended to the driver, and when he tried to wheedle a little extra out of me, I recalled, to my great annoyance, that I had only two and a half rubles left. If all the cheap rooms were taken, I would be fifty kopecks short. Paying him at last, I went over to Zinochka. I could tell by the way she was tugging at her handbag and twitching her shoulder that she was annoyed and that it would take some coaxing for me to budge her from the spot. The driver had disappeared, leaving behind the flat circle his sleigh had made in the snow as it turned sharply on its axis. The two curious passersby who had stopped to watch us enter the courtyard had now come in themselves and were standing a short way off, observing the proceedings. Positioning myself in such a way as to cut off Zinochka's view of them and putting my arm around her shoulders, I called her my sweet, my pet, my little darling, words that would have lost all their meaning had they not been said in a voice so sweet and cloying as to be the very essence of treacle.

As soon as I felt her give in, return to her former self—not so much the one who had given me an awesome look (or what I took for one) while we passed the Monastery of the Passion as the one who had said in the park, "Oh, how marvelous! How marvelous!"—I began a rather muddled, incoherent explanation of how, though I had a hundred-ruble note in my pocket, there was little likelihood of my finding change for it inside, and so I wondered if she could lend me just fifty kopecks which I would return in a matter of minutes. . . . Without letting me finish, she quickly, almost fearfully, opened a little simulated-crocodile oilcloth purse and emptied it into the cup of my hand. What I saw was a small mound of tiny silver five-kopeck pieces, the kind that had become something of a collector's item. I looked up at her questioningly.

"There are exactly ten of them," she said to set my mind at rest and, hunching up self-effacingly, apologetically, she added, "I've been collecting them for a long time now; people say they bring luck."

"But Zinochka, my pet," I said in noble indignation, "what a shame! Here, take them back. I can do without them."

Now truly annoyed and frowning with the effort of closing my big hand with her little ones, she insisted, "No, you take them. You must. You don't want to insult me, do you?"

Will she, won't she? Will she, won't she? was all

I could think or feel; it occupied my entire being as I guided Zinochka to the main entrance. On the first step she seemed to come to, and paused, miserable, to look back at the open gateway, where the two passersby had stood firm, like guards barring the way; then, as though we were still about to part, she looked up at me with a pitiful smile, looked down, and finally, stooping slightly, covered her face with her hands. I gripped her under the arms, pulled her up the stairs, and pushed her into the door, which was obligingly held open by the porter.

When an hour or so later we came out into the courtyard again, I asked Zinochka what direction she lived in, intending to tell her I lived in the opposite direction and take my leave of her in the gateway, the standard practice at Vinogradov's.

But whereas these definitive leave-takings were usually the result of boredom, satiety, and an occasional admixture of repulsion, feelings that supported my belief (no matter how I might regret it the next day) that the girl in question could never again be desirable, my farewell to Zinochka afforded nothing but frustration. Frustration because upstairs in the room, behind the screen, Zinochka, whom I had just contaminated, had fallen short of my expectations; she had remained as elated, and consequently sexless, as when she had said "Oh, how marvelous!" Once undressed, she began stroking my cheeks and murmuring "Oh, my little lovey-dovey, my little sweetheart" in a voice full of childish, infantile tenderness, a tenderness that had nothing flirtatious about it but that, because it came from the heart, disturbed my conscience and prevented me from delivering myself up wholly to what is usually called "shamelessness." (The word is misleading, however, the principal and most passionate trait of human depravity lying in the violation of shame, not in its absence.)

Without realizing it, Zinochka had prevented the beast from overcoming the man and therefore provoked a reaction of disappointment and frustration that led me to qualify the entire incident as wasteful. It was wasteful of me to contaminate the girl, I thought and felt, but what I meant by the word "wasteful" was not that I had committed a horrible act; on the contrary, what I meant was that I had made a sacrifice, hoping to gain a certain pleasure in return, which pleasure had not been forthcoming.

And not until I stood in the gateway and Zinochka found a safe place for the slip of paper on which I had jotted a made-up name and random telephone number, not until Zinochka thanked me, said good-bye, and started to walk away, yes, not until then did a voice inside me make itself heard. It was not the self-assured, insolent voice with which I addressed the world in my daydreams, on my couch, but the mild, even meek, voice I used when talking to myself. "Shame on you," it said caustically, "ruining a girl like that. Look at her. There she goes, the poor thing. Remember what she called you? 'My little lovey-dovey?' What did you do it for, anyway? What did she do to you? Shame on you!"

An amazing sight—the back of a person unjustly hurt moving off into the distance forever. There is a kind of human impotence in it, a frailty that calls out for pity, beckons you, makes you want to follow. There is something in that rear view which reminds you of injustices and offenses that need talking over and a different good-bye, need them now, at once, because a person is leaving forever and will leave much grief behind him, cause much anguish thereby, and perhaps rob others of sleep in their old age.

The snow had begun to fall again—a dry, cold snow. The wind shook even the streetlamps, and the shadows of the trees along the boulevard waved in concert like plumes. Zinochka had long since turned the corner, Zinochka had long since disappeared, but again and again I conjured her up, let her go as far as the corner, watched the back of her moving off; then, back first, she would fly to me once more. And when, absentmindedly slipping my hand into my pocket and hearing the clink of the ten silver five-kopeck pieces I had not in the end needed, I recalled her lips and her child-like voice saying "I've been collecting them for a long time now; people say they bring luck," it was like a whip lashing at my ignominious heart, a whip constraining me to run, run after Zinochka, run through the deep snow in that weakened, tearful state that comes from running after the last train of the day, knowing all the while it is out of reach.

Late into the night I wandered through the boulevards. I vowed to keep Zinochka's silver kopecks all my life, as long as I lived. As for Zinochka herself, I never saw her again. For Moscow is vast, and many are the people who dwell within her confines.

3

The leading lights of our class were Stein, Yegorov, and—or so I wished to believe at the time—myself.

I was friends with Stein, though I constantly had the uneasy feeling that the moment I stopped forcing myself to be friendly I would despise him. White-haired, browless, and prematurely balding, Stein was the son of a rich Jewish furrier. He was also the best student in the class. The teachers very rarely called on him, confident of his knowledge after years of impeccable responses. Whenever a teacher glanced down at his roster and came up with the name S-s-stein, a special silence would fall over the class. Extricating himself from the desk with a din that seemed to indicate someone was holding him back, Stein would scramble out into the aisle and, balancing precariously on his long, spindly legs, take up a position far back from the teacher's podium and at such an angle to the floor that if a straight line had been drawn from his toes to the ceiling it would have cut directly through his thin and narrow shoulders at the point where his enormous white hands were clasped as if in prayer. His lopsided posture—he leaned all his weight on one leg, barely touching the floor with the tip of the other shoe—gave the impression that one leg was longer than the other and made him look like a deformed old crone.

Awkward as he was, he was not in the least ridiculous. Listening to the questions, he affected disdain and indulgence; drumming out the answers, he rushed giddily ahead, propelled, it would seem, by an excess of knowledge. Anticipating the benevolent "You may return to your seat," he always tried to look past the class, out of the window, moving his lips as if chewing or whispering. Later, having scrambled back to his seat along the slippery parquet floor and sat down with the usual din, he would immediately start scribbling or rummaging in his desk until the class was distracted by the next question.

If someone told a funny story during the break and Stein happened to be sitting at his desk during the moment of general hilarity, he would fling back his head, shut his eyes, and wrinkle up his face to show what he was going through inside, at the same time pounding the desk over and over with the side of his hand, as if to dissipate the laughter threatening to smother him. Yet his lips would remain sealed, emitting not a sound, until the very last, when the laughter of the others had died down and he would open his eyes, wipe them with a handkerchief, and utter a "Whew."

His passions, which he talked about constantly, were the ballet and the "house" run by Marya Ivanovna in Kosoy Lane. His favorite expression was "We must be Europeans." He would use it all the time, pertinently or impertinently. "We must be Europeans," he would say to cap his account of an evening at the ballet in an expensive box adjacent to the stage. "We must be Europeans," he would repeat, hinting that after the ballet he had paid a visit to Marya Ivanovna's. Not until Yegorov began to harass him did he stop using it quite so often.

The son of a Kazan lumber merchant, Yegorov was also rich. He was always well groomed and well scented, and wore his shiny yellow hair parted in a gash to the neck and slicked down as if lacquered, so that it came undone in layers. He would have been handsome had it not been for his eyes, which were round and watery, the glass eyes of a bird; they made him look frightened and amazed whenever his face took on a serious expression. During his first few months at the school he went out of his way to emulate a man of the people, even styling himself Yagorushka. When someone shortened it to Yag, the name stuck.

Yag had been sent to Moscow at the age of fourteen, and so he entered the school as a fourth-year student. When our teacher showed him into the room one morning before classes and asked him to read the prayer, twenty-five pairs of probing eyes prepared to find something to mock at.

The prayer was usually read in a garbled monotone, which we associated with the time-honored ritual of getting out of our seats, standing for thirty seconds, and rattling the desks as we took our seats again. But Yag began the prayer with clarity and a kind of unnatural sincerity, crossing himself not as if he were swatting a fly from his nose as we did, but fervently, with his eyes shut, bowing theatrically and throwing his head back to fix the class icon, high up on the wall, with his dim eyes. The sniggers were not long in coming: we all suspected a joke, and our suspicion turned to certitude—and the sniggers to choral belly laughs—when Yag stopped short in the middle of the prayer and looked up at us, frightened and amazed. By then the teacher was so upset that he shouted at both Yag and the rest of us that if anything of the sort ever happened again he would bring the matter up with the school disciplinary council.

A week later, when everyone had learned that Yag came from an extremely religious family which had once belonged to a sect of the Old Believers, the same elderly teacher suddenly went up to Yag after classes, took his hand, and, blushing like a callow youth, said brusquely, "Yegorov, I want you to forgive me," and without another word tore his hand away and walked off down the corridor, completely stooped over, swinging his arms as if trying to grab something from the ceiling and toss it to the ground. Yag, meanwhile, went over to the window and stood with his back to us, blowing his nose for a long time.

But that was only at first. In later years Yag went into what the administration termed "a serious decline." After taking to drink, the first thing he would do upon entering class in the morning was to make a detour to Stein's desk and belch at him menacingly, filling his nose with fumes as with the smoke of a fragrant cigar. "We must be Europeans," he would tell us by way of explanation. Although Yag lived on his own in Moscow—renting a costly suite in a townhouse and obviously receiving ample funds from home, enough to make frequent appearances in fancy cabs in the company of women—he kept up with his lessons and did so well he was considered one of the best students. Few of us knew he had tutors for nearly every subject.

It might be said that the rest of the class adhered to the three of us—Stein, Yag, and me, or "the leading triumvirate," as we were called—the way the ends of a horseshoe adhere to a magnetized bar. At one end of the horseshoe we were coupled with the better students, at the other—moving along the semi-circle of descending marks—with the class dunce and ne'er-do-well. We, the leading triumvirate, combined, as it were, the basic traits of both: the high marks of the former with the bad reputation (in the eyes of the administration) of the latter.

On the side of the good students we were closest to Eisenberg, on the side of the mischiefmakers—to Takadzhiev.

Eisenberg, or Eisenberg the Meek, as we called him, was a modest, very diligent, very shy Jewish boy with a strange habit: before speaking or responding to a question in class, he would swallow his saliva, helping it down by tipping back his head, and then say something that sounded like *mte*. We all thought it essential to make fun of his sexual continence (not that we had any way of verifying it or that he himself ever confirmed it), and a crowd would surround him during the break and taunt him by shouting "Hey, Eisenberg! Show us your latest mistress" and looking pointedly at his hands. Whenever he spoke to one of us, he would lower his nettle-colored eyes, cock his head in the other direction, and cover his mouth with his hand.

Takadzhiev, an Armenian, was the oldest and most physically mature member of the class. He was loved by one and all for his phenomenal skill at shifting the butt of a teacher's ridicule from himself to the bad mark he had received; moreover, in contrast to the rest of us, he never showed the slightest animosity towards the teacher and always laughed longest and loudest at any joke. Like Stein he had a pet expression. It arose in the following way.

One day our literature teacher Semyonov, a kindhearted soul, was handing back exercise books, and when he came to Takadzhiev's he announced with an impish gleam in his eye that although the composition Takadzhiev had submitted was excellent and contained only a single piddling mistake, a misplaced comma, he was forced to give him a zero, and on account of that comma alone. The reason for what at first glance appeared a grossly unfair procedure was that Takadzhiev's composition corresponded word for word with Eisenberg's, yes, down to—and this was especially mysterious—the misplaced comma. Concluding his announcement with a favorite expression of his own—"You can tell the falcon by its flight and the stalwart by his snivel"—Semyonov handed Takadzhiev back his exercise book.

Instead of going back to his seat, however, Takadzhiev remained standing in front of the podium and asked Semyonov whether he had understood him correctly, whether it was possible for the two misplaced commas to have corresponded quite so exactly. When Semyonov gave him Eisenberg's composition for comparison, he leafed through them both for a long time, comparing and checking, a look of puzzlement spreading over his face until finally, in complete and utter amazement, he looked up at the class, which was on the verge of riotous laughter, turned ever so slowly, wide-eyed, to Semyonov, and, raising his shoulders and lowering the corners of his mouth, whispered tragically, "Well, watt ya know!" The zero had been entered, the price paid; Takadzhiev, who spoke perfectly normal

Russian, had simply taken advantage of the situation to entertain his friends, himself, and, in fact, the teacher, who, despite the harsh cruelty of his marks, loved a good laugh.

Such were our points of contact with the extremities of the class horseshoe. The closer the students moved to the middle, the duller they became—engaged as they were in the eternal battle between "Poor" and "Fair"—and the less we had to do with them.

In that far-off, alien territory of the middle lived a short, shockheaded, and acne-prone student by the name of Vasily Burkewitz. Then one day Burkewitz had a highly unusual adventure—one that deeply shook the quiet, ordered routine of our venerable institution.

4

It happened during our fifth year, in German class. The teacher, a certain von Volkmann who was completely bald and had a red face and reddish-white Mazeppa-like mustachios, had called on Burkewitz and was quizzing him in place, but when someone insisted on prompting in a loud whisper, von Volkmann lost his temper—his face turning from carrot-red to beet-red—and ordered Burkewitz to leave his seat and go to the blackboard. "*Verdammte Bummelei,*" he muttered, tugging lovingly at his reddish-white mustache, the safety valve of his ire.

Standing at the blackboard, Burkewitz was about to recite the lesson when suddenly something extremely disagreeable happened: he sneezed, sneezed in so inauspicious a manner as to eject a stream of mucus that plunged nearly to his waist and, once suspended there, began swinging back and forth. The class let out a titter.

"*Was ist denn wieder los?*" von Volkmann asked. Then, turning and seeing for himself, he said to Burkewitz, "*Na, ich danke.*"

Flushing blood-red, a red that soon paled to green, Burkewitz tore through his pockets with trembling hands. He had not, it turned out, brought a handkerchief.

"I say, old boy," Yag called out, "would you mind doing something about those oysters of yours. Christ! We've still got to eat lunch today."

"Well, watt ya know!" Takadzhiev chimed in, wide-eyed; by which time the whole class was howling with laughter.

At his wit's end and pitiful beyond measure, Burkewitz fled into the corridor. Von Volkmann, tapping his pencil against the desk, kept shouting "*R-r-ruhe,*" but all that came through the general pandemonium was the growl of the initial consonant, a sound remarkably illustrative of the expression in his eyes, which were bulging out so far that we were more afraid for him than for ourselves.

Next day, however, von Volkmann appeared in capital spirits and, game for a bit of amusement, called on Burkewitz again. "*Übersetzen Sie weiter,*" he said, but then added, in mock terror, "*aber selbstverständlich nur im Falle, wenn Sie heute ein Taschentuch besitzen.*"

After this quip von Volkmann launched into a series of gurgles, burbles, and wheezes. One of his odd points was that without a knowledge of the circumstances one was hard put to determine whether he was coughing or laughing. Now, watching his mouth open wide, the reddish tips of his mustache curl upward as if a mighty gale had just issued from his lips, and his bald head, raspberry-red by then, sprout a violet vein the size of a pencil, the entire class was convulsed with wild laughter. Stein, in the meantime, had thrown his head back and, eyes shut tight with suffering, was pounding a white fist on the desk. Not until the laughter had completely calmed down did he wipe his eyes and let out his "Whew."

It took several months for us to comprehend how cruel, misplaced, and unjust our laughter had been.

On the day of his misadventure Burkewitz did not come back to class, and the next day, the day of von Volkmann's German quip about handkerchiefs at the ready, he returned with a new face, a face of wood. From that day on we as a class ceased to exist for him. It was as if he had buried us. And we would probably have forgotten about him before long if a week or two later both we and our teachers had not noticed something extraordinarily strange: Burkewitz, "poor" to "fair" Burkewitz, had suddenly, unexpectedly, begun to make headway along the class horseshoe—slowly at first, then gaining speed—in the direction of Eisenberg and Stein.

The reason progress was slow and painful to begin with was that, marks or no marks, teachers are generally guided not so much by the knowledge a pupil demonstrates when called upon in class as by the reputation he has made for himself over the years. On the rare occasions when Stein or Eisenberg gave a weak answer, an answer for which Takadzhiev would definitely have received a "fair," they, who had acquired a reputation for brilliance, would be given, if grudgingly, the usual "outstanding."

Of course blaming teachers for playing favorites

is no more or less valid than blaming the world for playing favorites. How often do we find, say, artists with "outstanding" reputations receiving one ecstatic review after another for work which is weak and sloppy and which, had it been done by someone without a name, would have received no more than Takadzhiev's "fair." And Burkewitz had a greater obstacle than anonymity to surmount, for with the years he had acquired a reputation for mediocrity. That more than anything was what held him back. It blocked his way like a brick wall.

In time, of course, things changed. In evaluation procedure moving from "fair" to "good" is, psychologically, like crossing an ocean, while moving from "good" to "outstanding" is like crossing the street. But Burkewitz kept plugging away. Slowly, doggedly, never giving an inch, he crept up the horseshoe, closer to Eisenberg, closer to Stein. By the end of the school year (the sneezing incident had taken place in January) he was hot on Eisenberg's trail and with a little more time would surely have caught up with him. Still, when Burkewitz went off to the cloakroom after the last exam, wooden-faced as ever and not about to say good-bye to any of us, we had no idea that from the first days of the new school year we were to witness a fierce pitched battle for supremacy.

5

The battle began immediately. On one side Vasily Burkewitz, on the other—Eisenberg and Stein. To an outsider the competition would undoubtedly have appeared absurd: like Eisenberg and Stein, Burkewitz had by then a perfect record of "outstandings." And yet the battle was on—and a tense and heated battle it was, especially considering that the prize was no more than an invisible plus after the "outstanding," that something extra which, though impossible to enter in the class roster, would be keenly felt by both students and teachers and therefore indicate who was actually on top.

The history teacher followed the competition with special avidity, going so far as to call on all three—Eisenberg, Stein, and Burkewitz—one after the other for the same question. I shall never forget our charged silence, our thirsty, burning eyes, our concealed (and thus all the more intense) excitement. It seemed to me that what we experienced in that classroom was akin to what we might have experienced at a bullfight had we been deprived of the possibility of shouting out our emotions.

First came Eisenberg. Miniature workhorse that he was, he knew everything, everything we were required to know and then some. But just as the knowledge required for the lesson of the day amounted, in his rendition, to an irreproachably accurate, irreproachably precise, irreproachably meticulous, yet undeniably dry enumeration of historical events, so the knowledge not required for the lesson—the knowledge he trotted out to add luster to his response—amounted to little more than a chronological anticipation of the lessons to come.

Then up scrambled Stein, setting the room at an angle with his oblique posture. The question repeated, he drummed out a masterly answer. Gone was Eisenberg with his gulps of saliva and hesitant *mte*'s at the head of every sentence. Indeed, in some ways Stein's presentation could be called brilliant. He hummed along like a powerful motor, flashing foreign words like so many sparks, advancing full speed ahead through Latin quotations as through smooth tunnels, rapping out his words in a manner which, by obviating the necessity to strain and concentrate, left us free to bask in them, though not a single drop of sound fell into the void. And to crown it all, he launched into a brilliant peroration, the point of which was to demonstrate in no uncertain terms that though he, Stein, was required to deliberate on history, he actually misprized, looked down upon people of earlier times; that he, a man of the twentieth century, who had motorcars and aeroplanes, central heating and the Compagnie Internationale des Wagons-Lits at his disposal, considered himself fully justified in turning his nose up at people of the horse-and-buggy days; and that if he deigned to study them it was only to reinforce his already strong belief in the grandeur of our age of invention.

And finally, Vasily Burkewitz. And once more the question the other two had answered. At first we found him disappointing: he was too dry in his introductory remarks; our ears had been spoiled by Stein's drumbeat. But the first few sentences out of the way, he casually inserted a minor detail from the everyday life of the period in question, as if raising his hand and dropping a rose in full bloom over the mounds of history's monuments. On the heels of this first domestic detail came a second, still solitary, like a raindrop before a storm, then a third, then a multitude, until finally they formed a steady downpour that brought the sequence of events grinding to a halt. History's monuments, refurbished, so to speak, by the flowers now decorating them, seemed suddenly fresh, recent, unforgotten, newly dug. And that was only the beginning.

By bringing us in direct contact with old houses, the people who lived in them, and the activities they indulged in, he immediately gave the lie to Stein's standpoint, which glorified our age over the past for no other reason than that the distance covered in twenty hours by our deluxe express trains took more than a week to cover by pony express. Skillfully (yet without a hint of premeditation) juxtaposing present and past forms of everyday life, Burkewitz made it clear, though not in so many words, that Stein was under a misapprehension: that the difference between people living in the horse-

and-buggy days and people living now in the era of technological achievement—a difference that Stein believed gave him, a man of the twentieth century, the right to set himself up over people of past eras—is in fact no difference at all. And not only that there is no difference between the two but that this very lack of difference is the only way to explain the striking similarity in human relations between the days when it took a week to go a certain distance and the present, when it takes only twenty hours. That just as now very rich people in expensive clothes travel in international sleeping-cars, so then richly dressed people, people swathed in sable, rode in silk-upholstered coaches; that just as now people not quite so richly dressed but in perfectly decent clothes, whose goal in life is to travel in international sleeping-cars, travel second-class, so then there were people who rode in less fancy coaches and wore fox, but dreamed of acquiring a fancier coach and exchanging their fox furs for sable; that just as now there are people who travel third-class, unable to afford an express ticket and therefore condemned to suffer the slow train's plank seats, so then there were people without rank or money who spent long post-house nights on bedbug-infested couches; that, finally, just as now there are people who tramp along the tracks, hungry, miserable, and in rags, so then there were people just as hungry, miserable, and raggedy, tramping along the post road. The silks have long since rotted, the coaches crumbled and wasted away, the sables been ravished by moths, but people—they might as well be the very same individuals who had never died—have entered today's world with identical petty vanities, envies, and enmities. So much for Stein's storybook past, a past made obsolete by locomotives and electricity; pulled into focus by the force of Burkewitz's arguments, the past began to take on the clear-cut contours of the present. And obstinately going back over the events and everyday details he had spoken of at the start, and confidently linking them to the characters and activities of concrete individuals, Burkewitz won us over to his side. After numerous acute juxtapositions, all the more convincing for his refusal to formulate a definite pronouncement about them, the curve of Burkewitz's argument led inexorably to a conclusion he yet left for us to reach, namely, that in the past, in the distant past, we could scarcely fail to notice a repugnant, sacrilegious injustice: the *disparity* between the vices of some and the virtues of others and between the sables draping some and the rags draping others. In the past, that is. He made no reference at all to the present, as though taking for granted how perfectly well we were all aware of the repugnant disparity in the world of today. But the spider had spun its web. Surely, inexorably following Burkewitz along the zigzags of its sturdy steel bars, we arrived at the unshakable conviction that life was easier for the foolish than the wise, better for the scheming than the frank, freer for the greedy than the kind, more gratifying for the cruel than the weak, more luxurious for the powerful than the meek, more comfortable for the lying than the just, more pleasurable for the sensual than the chaste; that thus it had been and thus it would remain as long as man walked the earth.

The class held its breath. There were nearly thirty people in the room, and I could distinctly hear my neighbor's pocket watch—possession of which was forbidden by the administration—illicitly ticking away. On the podium the history teacher kept his red eyelashes pointed down at the class roster, making an occasional face or running his fingers through his beard as if to say, "A queer customer that one."

Burkewitz ended his presentation with a reference to a disease that had been evolving through the ages and that was gradually taking over mankind, a disease that in our age of technological progress, had succeeded in contaminating man everywhere—the disease known as vulgarity. For it was vulgarity that made man react with scorn to everything he did not understand, and it grew deeper and deeper with the growing fatuity and triviality of the objects and ideas that prompted his admiration.

We understood. Here was a stone cast in the face of his predecessor Stein, who, the moment he realized all eyes were on him, had ducked into his desk as if looking for something.

We understood something else as well: that the centuries-old and seemingly hopeless injustice of human relations Burkewitz had alluded to provoked neither despair nor fury in him but served as a kind of fuel, a fuel prepared especially to flow into his innermost self and, far from exploding destructively, to burn there with a steady, calm, yet powerful fire. Looking at those dirty, down-at-the-heel shoes; those baggy, threadbare trousers; those broad, billiard-ball cheeks, tiny gray eyes, and chocolate locks, we all had the feeling—a keen, irresistible feeling—that within him seethed the terrible Russian power which knows no block or barrier or any impediment whatever: a power of steel, solitary and morose.

6

The battle among Burkewitz, Stein, and Eisenberg, which Stein caustically dubbed "the Battle of the White and Soiled Roses," and in which Burkewitz's absolute superiority was soon recognized by all, came to an abrupt halt one day when the class voiced its feeling aloud and as one.

It happened quite by chance. One morning early in November, when all the students were sitting at their desks waiting for the history teacher, an eighth-year student strode into our room with such determination that the entire class took him for the teacher and rose accordingly. The general outbreak of vivid and eloquent expletives was such that the student, brazenly mounting the teacher's podium and raising his arms, intoned, "Excuse me, gentlemen, but can you tell me where I am? Is this a cell for common criminals who've mistaken one of their own for the prison warden, or the sixth-year class of one of Moscow's finest classical secondary schools?" The class sat down again.

"Gentlemen," he went on, dead serious, "may I have your attention for a moment? The Minister of Education has arrived in Moscow this morning, and there is reason to believe he will be paying us a visit some time tomorrow. I don't suppose I need to tell you—you know it perfectly well yourselves—that the impression the Minister takes with him from these halls is of the utmost importance for our school. Nor need I tell you that the headmaster's office, though deeming it utterly inconceivable to negotiate with us as concerns possible preparation for the visit, would nonetheless look favorably upon any preparation we might undertake on our own. May I therefore ask you, gentlemen, to give me the name of your best student? He will join us at a small gathering this evening, and tomorrow, as your delegate, inform you of the decisions taken. All of you who wish to maintain the long-lived and as yet unsullied reputation of our glorious school will then stand by them unconditionally."

This said, he lifted an open notebook to his clearly quite nearsighted eyes and, poising his pencil over the page and blinking his eyes as one does when awaiting a sound, added, "Well? The name?"

In a hum of voices that beat against the windowpanes like hundreds of ill-tempered flies, the class called out unanimously, "Bur-ke-witz!" and a well-wisher from the back tacked on affectionately, "Stand up, Vaska!" though there was no reason for him to stand or place for him to go. The student noted the name, thanked the class, and hurried off. The game was lost, the battle done. Burkewitz was in first place.

And as if aware the competition had come to an end (though perhaps for reasons of his own), the history teacher marched into the room and, taking his seat with an irritated shuffle of the feet, called immediately on Burkewitz to recite the lesson for the day. "And may I a-ask you," he added, "to ke-e-ep to the curri-i-culum as it sta-a-nds."

Burkewitz understood. He recited the lesson for the day and recited it in the spirit of the curriculum as it stood, in the spirit of the unsullied honor of our glorious school, and in the spirit of the Minister of Education, who that very morning had arrived in Moscow.

7

"If that snivel hadn't made a man of me, I'd have grown up a sniveler instead," Burkewitz once said to me. But that was much later, in our last days at school, when we were taking the final round of exams and the school priest scandal had brought us a bit closer.

Until that point Burkewitz had exchanged not a word with me or anyone else, had treated us as strangers. The single exception, outside the necessities imposed by normal scholastic intercourse, consisted of the words he had with Stein on the following occasion:

One day, during the main break, a group of students surrounded Stein and struck up a conversation about ritual murders, in the course of which someone asked him with a cruel smile whether he, Stein, believed in the possibility of their existence. The smile Stein flashed back was a heartrending sight. "We Jews," he answered, "do not like to spill human blood. We prefer sucking it. What can you expect, after all? We must be Europeans."

At that moment Burkewitz, who happened to be standing nearby, turned to Stein for the first time in his life and said to everyone's great surprise, "If I am not mistaken, Mr. Stein, you are afraid to face up to anti-Semitism. Your fears are unwarranted. Anti-Semitism is far from frightening; it is merely repulsive, pitiful, and stupid: repulsive because it is directed against the tribe rather than the individual, pitiful because it is envious where it would appear to be derisive, stupid because it consolidates what it purports to destroy. Jews will cease to be Jews only when being a Jew means not so much accepting persecution in secular affairs as accepting defeat in affairs of morality. And that defeat will come only when our Christians become true Christians at last—in other words, men who deliberately sacrifice the comforts in their lives so as to better the lives of others, and who derive pleasure and joy from so doing. But that has not happened yet, and two millennia do not appear to have sufficed. Which is why I say you are misguided, Mr. Stein, when you try to purchase a questionable dignity by debasing before these swine the people to which you have the honor—the honor, do you hear?—to belong. And I hope you feel properly ashamed that it is I, a Russian, telling all this to you, a Jew."

Like the others I stood motionless, in silence. And for the first time in my life I, like the others, seemed to feel a sharp, sweet pride in the knowledge that I was a Russian and that we Russians could boast of at least one Burkewitz amongst us. Why I suddenly felt it, where it came from, I could not tell. I only knew that before I had even grasped the meaning of the few words Burkewitz had uttered I could sense in them a special kind of chivalry, a chivalry of self-humiliation in defense of a poor, hapless alien, a chivalry towards non-Russian nationalities that was so characteristically Russian. And since no one attacked Burkewitz, since the crowd surrounding Stein quickly dispersed, apparently unwilling to take part in an affair beneath its dignity, and since several voices called out, "That's right, Vaska," "Well put," and "Good for you, Vaska," I had the feeling that the others had had the same reaction and that they were praising Burkewitz for the sense of national pride he had instilled in them with his words. Stein himself, of course, did not, could not share that reaction, and turning away abruptly with a smile full of rage, he went over to Eisenberg, slipped his enormous white fingers under the belt of Eisenberg's school uniform, pulled him up close, and began telling or asking him something in a low voice.

For the next few minutes I experienced a kind of antipathy towards Stein. It did not last long, however; I realized that on the day my mother had come to school with the envelope, I too had acted like Stein, renouncing her in the hope of preserving my dignity; that if on that day Burkewitz had come up to me and said that a son ought to be ashamed of renouncing his mother merely because she was old and ugly and dressed in rags, that indeed he owed her more respect the more aged, more decrepit, and more raggedy she became—if something of the sort had happened during the break that day, then my schoolmates who had asked me who that clown was, that clown in a petticoat, would most likely have agreed with Burkewitz, whereas I, I in my moment of shame, would quite naturally have felt not the love for my mother those outsiders wished to impose on me but a hatred for the busybody behind it all.

And moved by the feelings we thus shared, I went up to Stein and, putting my arm firmly around his waist, started off down the corridor with him.

8

The war with Germany had been raging for over a year and a half, but two weeks before the final round of examinations was due to begin, all my close friends at school, and I myself, completely lost interest in it.

I still remembered how excited I had been in the days immediately following the declaration of war. The excitement had made me exuberant, intrepid; it filled me, in short, with great joy. I had spent all day walking through the streets, mingling, as at Eastertime, with the idle crowd and echoing its many and loud anti-German sentiments. But I did not vilify the Germans because I hated them; I vilified them because the harder I pounded away with my abuse and invective, the more deeply I experienced the exceedingly pleasant feeling of oneness with the crowd around me. If at the time someone had shown me a lever and told me that I could blow up all Germany by giving it a flick, that I could cripple the population and annihilate every living German with a flick of the wrist, I would have done so gladly, without a second thought, and then gone off to make my bows—so positive was I that if something of the sort could be achieved and was achieved, the crowd would burst into a paroxysm of rejoicing.

It must have been the spiritual contact, the syrupy feeling of oneness with the crowd that prevented my imagination from flaring up as it did several days later when, stretched out on the couch in the darkness of my tiny room, I pictured myself on a platform in the middle of a large teeming square where a pale German boy had been brought for me to execute. "Kill him," the crowd said—no, *ordered.* "Cut off his head! Kill him! Your life depends on it, the lives of your dear ones, your happiness, the future of your family. If you fail to kill him, we will kill you." But I, looking down at the little German towhead and into his watery, importunate eyes, hurled away my hatchet and said, "Do what you will. I refuse." And hearing my refusal, my magnanimous refusal, the crowd burst into wild and joyous applause. Such was the dream I had several days later.

But just as in my first fantasy, the one in which I annihilated sixty million people with the flick of a wrist, I was motivated not at all by a feeling of enmity towards the people involved but by the prospect of recognition for having achieved something significant, so in my refusal to cut off the head of the boy standing before me I was motivated not so much by a respect for human life as again by the desire to point up my exceptional nature by bringing upon myself the ultimate penalty.

Within a month my ardor for the war had cooled, and if I preserved a kind of lukewarm enthusiasm for reports in the papers about how the Russians had defeated the Germans in one or another battle, grumbling to myself, "Serves the bastards right—what made them poke their noses into our affairs?", then a few weeks later, reading about one or another victory of the Germans over the Russians, I would grumble to myself, "Serves the bastards right—what made us get mixed up with the Germans?" And when, a few weeks after that, a boil cropped up on my nose, it engaged and provoked and exasperated me if not more than, then at any rate more sincerely than, the entire world war.

All words like war, victory, defeat, the dead, the captured, the wounded—all those ghastly words which in the early days of the war felt as vibrant and alive as live carp in one's hands—they were all, for me at least, suddenly drained of the blood they had been written in, and deprived of that blood, they turned into mere printer's ink. They were like a burnt-out bulb: the switch kept clicking, but the light never flashed; the words kept coming, but no image emerged. I could no longer comprehend how the war could continue to stir people it did not directly touch.

Since at that point Burkewitz had had absolutely no contact with me or anyone in our class for three years, we could not, of course, know what he thought of the war, yet we were certain that his stance did not differ from ours. The fact that Burkewitz had failed to attend the victory prayers in the main assembly hall went unnoticed and was recalled only later, after the incident with the priest. As for his constant absences from the by then months-old course in military training, they were put down either to his ill health or to his reluctance to yield first place even in physical prowess to the remarkably hale and hearty but otherwise hopeless Takadzhiev.

And even as I witnessed the terrible confrontation that had to come, I did not realize in my ignorance that Burkewitz's words were merely the thunder following that flash of lightning which many years before had soared up over Tolstoy's estate, the "nest of gentlefolk" known as Yasnaya Polyana.

9

During that final year our literature class had to be canceled one day when the teacher fell ill. Trying to keep from disturbing the sixth- and seventh-year classes—their rooms were in the same wing of the building—we wandered quietly up and down the corridor. We had no supervision. The man who usually took charge in such instances had put us on our honor as "all-but's"—by which he meant we were all but enrolled at university—and slipped downstairs to the teachers' room. Most of us were in high spirits: the last round of examinations, the final stage of school, was to begin in a little over a week.

A small group of students had gathered at the

large three-paneled window next to the door, and Yag, in the center, was holding forth softly but with great animation. When one of the students tried to interrupt him with an objection, he was visibly annoyed and, forgetting the need to keep his voice down, let out a loud, obscene oath.

At that moment most of the group saw what was in store for Yag, and they re-formed ranks, from a circle facing Yag into a semi-circle facing the school priest. No one had noticed when or whence the priest had appeared.

"Where is your shame, my children?" said the priest, waiting until everyone was aware of his presence and addressing the group as a whole rather than anyone in particular. His voice was censorious and slightly unctuous, the voice of an old man. "Remember," he continued, "that in several years you will be entering the public life of our great country as responsible citizens. Remember that the disgraceful words I have just had the misfortune to hear mean something horrible. Remember that even if you are unconscious of their literal meaning as you say them, you are not justified in saying them; indeed, you are all the more to blame. For in so doing you demonstrate that you speak the horrible words in question every hour, every minute of the day, that you have ceased to look upon them as swearwords and use them merely to embellish your speech. Remember that you have had the good fortune to study the music of Pushkin and Lermontov, and it is that music our unfortunate Russia expects from you, that and none other."

As he spoke, the eyes of the students standing before him grew dull and impenetrable; they might have seemed devoid of all expression whatsoever were not the very absence of expression meant to express the conviction that since they had not been the ones to use the swearword, all the priest's reproaches had not the slightest bearing on them. But at the same time that boredom and indifference spread over *their* eyes and faces, Burkewitz's eyes lit up with a mischievous gleam, and his lips stretched into a thin, malicious smile. The priest's words—like so many needles aimed at the semicircle of stone eyes and faces, yet independent of the will behind the hand that cast them—gravitated to that smile as to a magnetic field. It was as if Burkewitz were the culprit and the words about Pushkin and Lermontov were directed entirely at him.

"It is obvious, Father," Burkewitz retorted in a soft but chilling voice, "that your acquaintance with Messrs. Pushkin and Lermontov is limited to the authorized anthologies, and that you deem any closer acquaintance—insofar as it might upset your present views—unnecessary."

"Yes," the priest responded firmly, "I find a limited acquaintance with them necessary for *you,* just as I find it necessary to cut the thorns from a rose before giving it to a child. So much for that. And now may I remind you that the swearwords I have just heard here are intolerable and unworthy of a Christian."

He made this last remark in a harsh voice, while adjusting the cross on his purple cassock with a slightly trembling hand.

Why does he keep standing there? I thought. Why doesn't he go away? But looking over at Burkewitz, I understood. Burkewitz's face had turned gaunt and gray, and had begun to twitch, but his eyes bored into the priest's face with keen hatred. He's going to strike him, I thought. Instead, Burkewitz jerked his arms back convulsively as if trying to catch someone behind him, then took a step forward, and—in unexpectedly determined, ringing tones—began to speak.

"Swearwords, as you have deigned to remark, are unworthy of a Christian. Granted. No one will argue with you there. But since you, God's servant, have undertaken to set us on the path of truth, you will not, I trust, take it amiss if I ask you where, when, and how you have proved yourself worthy of the Christian values which we lack and which you would inculcate in us. Where were you, may I ask, you and your Christian values, when ten months ago the streets of Moscow were swarming with bloodthirsty hordes waving colored rags—hordes of beings who call themselves human but whose dull-witted fury makes them unworthy of comparison with a herd of wild beasts—where were you, God's servant, on that day, so terrible for us all? What kept you, the champion of Christianity, from gathering us children, as you call us, from gathering us here, in these walls, in this building, where you have the audacity to teach us Christ's commandments? Why did you hold your tongue on that day—the day war was announced, the day fratricide was made into law—yet speak up here and now against a chance swearword? Is it not because fratricide does not contradict, does not contravene your understanding of Christian values so much as the oath you heard here today? Swearing in the form it takes here is indeed unworthy of a Christian, and you were right, perfectly right to raise your voice against it. But where have you been, God's servant, where have you been these past ten months, when every day, every minute, fathers have been torn forcibly from their children, boys from their mothers, and then once again sent by force into fire, murder, and death—where have you been all this time, and why haven't you protested against all these crimes in your sermons at least to the extent you protested here when confronted with a single oath? Why? Why? Is it not because all these horrors do not in the least contradict your Christian values? How can you, Christianity's noble guardian, having once walked through the school courtyard and seen our arms drill, our daily lesson in the art of fratricide, find the insolence to smile and give us encouraging nods of your holy head? Why these encouraging smiles, why this silence? Is it not because arms drills do not contravene your Christian values? How dare you disdain Him Whose bright name you use as both a cover and a justification for your pitiful life? How dare you pray, yes, pray for brother to conquer brother, brother to defeat brother, brother to kill brother? What enemy have you in mind this time? Surely not the one whom only a year ago you told us in your unctuous voice to forgive and love? Or perhaps the prayer for the conquest, defeat, murder, and annihilation of one man by another fits your understanding of Christian values all too nicely. Come to your senses! You're nothing but a petty church functionary grown fat and stupid at the people's expense! Come to your senses and stop seeking to vindicate your actions through those of fellow functionaries in faith who are risking their lives in the fields of horror, giving communion to the dying and comfort to the wounded. For they know as well as you that their mission, their Christian duty lies not so much with the ill and wounded as with the healthy on their way to slaughter. Do not, then, liken yourself to a doctor—unless, perhaps, to one who treats syphilitic sores with beauty cream—or seek to justify yourself by claiming to support a ghastly business such as this out of loyalty to the monarch and the government, or love for your country and its strength. Do not seek to justify yourself at all. For you know that your monarch is Christ, your country—the conscience, your government—the Gospel, your strength—love. Come to your senses, then, and act! Act because every minute is precious, because every minute, every second people are shooting, people are killing, people are falling. Come to your senses and act, because these people—and their mothers and fathers and children and brothers, everybody, everyone—expect you, yes, *you,* Christ's servants, who have fearlessly sacrificed your lives to Him, to intervene in this disgrace, to stand up among the madmen and cry out loudly, loudly because you are many, so many that you can cry out to the whole world, 'Throw down your arms, my people! Put an end to your slaughter!' That, yes, that and only that is your duty."

Watching Burkewitz—his head thrown back and one arm oddly swinging, his body quivering all over—stagger past us and through the entrance to the stairs, I had but a single thought: That's the end of you, Vaska. That's the end of you, poor thing.

Only then did I turn and see the purple cossack disappear with an elegant swish against the doorjamb.

And at that very instant, the instant we flung ourselves on one another, talking and gesticulating madly, a muffled din began swelling ominously from below and, like a wave washing up and into a seaside cottage, it rose higher and higher, rattling windows and walls and floor, until at last it burst with a deafening roar through the wide-open doors of our corridor, the doors to the sixth- and seventh-year rooms. Class was over.

10

To avoid entering into the details of so extraordinary an incident with the other classes, which had spilled into the corridor for the break, we went back into our room.

"The fellow's an idiot, an out-and-out idiot," said Stein, putting his white hand on Yag's shoulder. The black cloth made it look like a splash of cream.

"Keep out of this, Stein, will you?" Yag responded, pushing him away. "You're the European, after all, and this is an Asiatic affair. Try to understand: the Talmud has not been violated; there's nothing for you to be upset about." And waiting until Stein, rebuffed, had gone back to his desk, Yag turned to the group that had assembled excitedly near the window and said under his breath, "It never ceases to amaze me how our Jew boys worship the clergy. Heaven help you if you so much as touch a priest. You'll have the Yids on your back in no time."

"Well, watt ya know!" said Takadzhiev with a shake of the head, but they did not laugh. They were too much involved in a heated exchange of opinions. No one could finish a thought; the others kept butting in, challenging, disputing. Some said that Burkewitz was right, war was a disaster and of no use to anyone but generals and quartermasters. Others said that war was a fine thing, without wars there would be no Russia, it was time to stop dithering and fight. Still others said that although war was a horrible thing, we had been forced into it now, and if a surgeon lost his faith in medicine in the course of an operation he had no right to go off and abandon his patient before completing it. There were those who said that the whole thing was insane: surely no priest in a school in Berlin would have put up with a tirade like Burkewitz's; and those who said that although the war had been imposed on us and our reputation as a great power excluded all talk of peace, Burkewitz's basic idea was correct: clergymen the world over were bound by the universal principles of Christianity—the risk of persecution under martial law notwithstanding—to protest and fight against the continuation of the war.

Yag disagreed with the latter view. "Wait a minute," he said. "Just what Christian principles have you got in mind? If Burkewitz sets such great store by your Christian principles, then why, may I ask, hasn't he said a word to us for three years? Think of it—three years. And what harm did we do him with our little laugh? Good God, a horse would have laughed at that string of snot. So why has the great Christian been glowering at us for three years? Why is the mother———— always ready to sink his teeth into us? No, my friends, there's something else at work here. He needs war like the air he breathes. It's not Christianity he's after; it's an end to Christianity. That's what's got him up in arms, the bastard. That and nothing else."

Standing off to the side, I wondered how it had come about that Burkewitz—the best student in the class, the pride of the school, the only possible candidate for the gold medal—Burkewitz of all people was done for. That he was in fact done for was beyond all doubt, because that very day, that very moment, perhaps, the Academic Council would be summoned and would of course vote unanimously to expel him. The resulting black mark on his identification papers would haunt him the rest of his life. And good-bye, university—only ten days before examinations. I had always felt that the closer a person came to a goal that suddenly slipped out of reach the more keenly he experienced despair, though I was fully capable of understanding that a goal close at hand was not necessarily more attainable than a goal at a point farther in the distance. Here was where feeling fell away from reason, practice from theory—both co-existing on an equal basis, unable to make peace and merge or to acknowledge a victor.

Still, how could such a thing have happened to Burkewitz? And what was at work: premeditated malice or temporary insanity? I thought of the defiant smile that attracted the priest's brief diatribe against him and said to myself, premeditated malice; I thought of his trembling head and drunken step and changed my verdict to temporary insanity.

I had a strong need to see him, a need finely woven out of three distinct feelings: the first, a cruel desire to look in the face of someone who has just undergone a great misfortune; the second, the daring involved in associating with someone stamped as a pariah, as someone who had taken a step that no one in the class would ever dream of taking; the third, the one that provided the brawn for the other two—was a feeling of certitude that being seen near or even in conversation with Burkewitz could not possibly cause me problems with the administration.

The clock showed two minutes before the end of the break. Slipping out of the classroom, I elbowed my way along the corridor through the disorderly pounding of feet and the clamor of talking and yelling until I came to the staircase. When I closed the door behind me, the shouting and stomping fooled me by dying down for a moment; it returned soon enough, however, in a muted but dense hum.

I looked about me. One flight down, near the door to the "punishment cell," which, not having been used for ten years, had a rusty padlock on it, I saw Burkewitz sitting on the steps, his back to me. His legs were spread wide, his elbows rested on his knees, and his head lay cradled in his hands. Slowly and quietly, I tiptoed my way down the stairs, my eyes riveted upon his back, a back arched into a hump under the tightly stretched material of his shirt and bounded by the two sharp points of his shoulder blades. In that twisted back and those protruding shoulder blades I saw a combination of impotence, resignation, and despair.

Tiptoeing up from behind—he still could not see who I was—I laid my hand on his shoulder. He did not start, he did not uncover his face; his back arched slightly more—and that was all. Still staring down at him, I shifted my hand from his shoulder to his hair. The moment I touched his warm hair, I felt something move in me, something that would have filled me with shame had it been seen. Glancing back in a way that did not appear to be a glance and satisfied that the staircase was empty, I ran my hand gently through his coarse, chocolate-colored hair. It was pleasant. I suddenly felt so light and tender that I did it again and again. Without raising his face from his hands, and therefore unable to see who was stroking his hair, Burkewitz suddenly asked in a muffled voice, "Vadim?"

With a crystalline feeling of joy in my breast I immediately sat down beside him. Burkewitz had said *Vadim,* he had called me by name. And since he had done so without having seen me, it meant that for the first time in my life I had been noticed for the gentle, responsive nature of my heart rather than the flippant, heartless nature of my responses. My fingers tightened as they grasped the hot roots of his hair, and pulling his head out of the shell of his palms, I brought it up to mine, eye to eye. I peered into his small gray orbs. They were oddly distorted by the skin being drawn back to the point where I was holding his hair. For a moment they peered back into mine with a look of sullen suffering, but then, obviously unable to master the harsh male tears welling up inside them, they disappeared behind their lids on either side of the fierce cleft that had dug its way between his brows. All of a sudden, the moment the eyes fell shut, I heard an unfamiliar voice saying hoarsely, "Vadim . . . You . . . Kind . . . Only . . . Only one . . . Believe . . . So hard . . . I . . . From all . . . My heart . . . You believe . . ."

For the first time feeling myself embraced by strong male arms, feeling my back clasped tightly, my cheek pressed against a male cheek, I blurted out roughly, "Vasya . . . I'm . . . your . . . your . . ." "Friend" was what I meant to add, but while I might have got as far as "fr," I was afraid of bursting into tears by the time I reached the vowel. Instead, I gave Burkewitz a push hard enough to send his head reeling—with its closed eyes, short nose, and pallid complexion it looked like Beethoven's death mask—and, in complete awareness and apathetic terror of what I was about to do, I flung myself down the stairs, dashed down the stairs as one rushes off to fetch a doctor for a dying friend, not so much because the doctor can save him as because the action itself mitigates the desire that arises from the quite unbearable feeling of pity at seeing him suffer, the desire to experience his sufferings as well.

The staircase behind me, I matched my stride to the slippery blue-white tiles of the dining hall. A slice of sun from the window barely had time to graze my eyes before I plunged into the dark humidity of the cloakroom, my soles sticking to its asphalt floor as if permanently nailed down. Then up another staircase. I had my opening ready: "As a true Christian, I wish to bring to your attention . . ." The rest was unimportant, the rest would follow like clockwork. "Like clockwork, like clockwork." I took the steps three at a time, puffing "like clockwork" each time I put my foot down.

Climbing three steps at a time—especially the high steps at our school—forced me to bend far forward and keep my head low, so I did not notice that at the head of the stairs I had been observed and awaited by the serpentine eyes and black frock coat of the headmaster, Richard Sebastianovich Keimann. Not until I reached the final steps did I see the columns of his legs rise before my eyes—and then they stopped me in my tracks as surely as if they had been rifles shooting at me.

His raspberry face and black goatee gazed down on me for a time in silence. "Whoot seems to be the trouble?" he asked at last. The disdainful, hate-filled "whoot," pronounced by moving his lips from under his mustache as for a kiss, was the signal that for eight years had had the power to halt our heartbeat.

I was shamefully silent.

"Whoot seems to be the trouble?" Keimann repeated, his baritone rising to an anxious, solicitous tenor.

My arms and legs were trembling. A familiar block of ice had formed in my stomach. I remained silent.

"I want ta kna what tha trable as," Keimann shouted in what was by then a falsetto, which he could keep from breaking only by pronouncing all vowels as "a." His yap-like ejaculations bounced from one stone ceiling to the next, zigzagging their way up the marble staircase.

But while trying to use the breaks between the headmaster's squawks to reawaken the less and less comprehensible and all but moribund feeling of pity for Burkewitz that had landed me there, I felt a growing feeling of rage directed against crimson-faced Keimann. Moreover, while I was thrilled at the realization that my rage would provide me with the courage necessary to stand up to him and deliver the words I had planned to deliver, I also dimly realized that even if the words had remained the same, my change of heart had altered the reason for saying them: my original idea was to do harm to myself; now all I cared about was harming and offending Keimann. Using the expression of my face and the tone of my voice to give every word the force of a furious slap in the headmaster's crimson face, I began to speak: "As a true Christian, I am completely and utterly . . ."

At that very moment, nearly choking with hatred and rage, I was interrupted by the heat and weight of a hand on the back of my neck, and turning my head, I saw a purple chest with a gold cross rising and falling rapidly upon it.

"Please excuse the intrusion, Richard Sebastianovich," said the priest, whose heavily lined, snub-nosed face split and swam back and forth before my unfocused eyes, "but he was on his way to see me." And so saying, he put his arm around my shoulders. Then, with a quick glance in my direction and a significant squint in the direction of the headmaster, he added, "It's a small matter and has nothing to do with the school. I am the one he wanted to see."

All at once Keimann the headmaster turned into Keimann the roué. "By all means, Father, I had no idea. Forgive me, please." And making a grand "be my guest" sort of gesture, the sort of gesture a magnanimous host might use to usher his guests to the groaning board, he turned on his heel, unbuttoned his frock coat, put his hands in his pockets, and, sailing off as if to invite a lady to waltz with him, started up the marble steps.

Meanwhile, the priest had turned me round to face him and rested his hands on my shoulders, thereby uniting the two of us like a set of parallel bars hung with the pennants of his cassock's broad sleeves. I now stood with my back to Keimann, but by looking into the priest's eyes, which gazed off towards the staircase, I could tell that he was waiting for Keimann to turn the corner and disappear up the next stretch of stairs.

"Tell me," he said, moving his eyes from the staircase to my face at last, "tell me, my boy, what made you want to do it?" He gave my shoulders a slight squeeze as he said the word "it." Having calmed down, however, I was at a loss to respond.

"You are silent, my boy. Well then, allow me to

answer for you and say that you thought it inadmissible to stand by while your friend ruined himself, as you doubtless supposed, for Christ's truth, a truth far more precious to you than material comforts. Isn't that so?"

Although I could not help thinking that it was not so at all and that the very premise gave me a bad conscience, I was moved by a combination of courtesy and respect for the old man to nod my acquiescence.

"And having made up your mind to act," he went on, "you must have had no doubt whatsoever that the first thing I would do was to go and complain to the authorities, report on everything that had happened upstairs. Isn't that so, my boy?"

Although this premise corresponded much more closely to the truth than the first, the same combination of courtesy and respect kept me from making the very move they had induced in me the first time round, and instead of confirming his statement with a nod or facial expression, I merely looked him in the eye expectantly.

"In that case," said the priest, staring at me with his oddly dilated pupils, "in that case you were wrong, my boy. So go and find your friend and tell him that I am a priest not an informer, no." He gave my shoulders another squeeze. But then, as if turning feeble and decrepit on the spot and losing all self-confidence, he added in a dwindling voice, "And God . . . God be his judge for having offended an old man. You see, my son," he spoke so softly it seemed a secret, "in the war . . ." he barely whispered through the lips, "killed . . ."

When the priest first started speaking to me, the proximity of his bearded face and the weight of his arms on my shoulders had made me feel uneasy, as though he were trying to draw me to him. Now that those arms were pushing me away, I felt a sudden strong urge to move close to him. And just then he dropped his hands from my shoulders, tore his brimming, angry eyes away, and quickly moved off down the corridor.

Two feelings, two desires welled up in me: the first was to press my face against the priest's, kiss it, and dissolve into tender tears; the second was to run to Burkewitz, tell him everything, and dissolve into cruel laughter. The two desires were like perfume and putrefaction: instead of canceling each other, they enhanced each other, the only difference between them being that the desire to press my face against the priest's diminished in intensity as he disappeared down the corridor, while the nagging desire to blurt out the joyful news, to play the hero, gained in intensity as I rushed back to Burkewitz. And though perfectly aware that haste impairs heroic dignity, I was unable to restrain myself, and blabbed everything in a few short words the moment I came within range.

But clearly Burkewitz did not understand. He gazed up at me with a distant look, a look of tortured exhaustion in his eyes, and asked me absentmindedly—out of politeness, it seemed—to start again. Then, much more calmly, I went into everything in great detail. And as I spoke, I observed something in him that I had once observed in two chess players I happened to be watching. While one of them, hunched over the board, plotted his next move, the other, completely oblivious of the board and apparently upset or indignant over something, carried on an animated conversation with the people sitting beside him. When he was interrupted to be told his opponent had made a move, he cut the conversation short and turned to the board. At first his eyes still shone with the tail end of the ideas he had left unsaid, but the longer he looked at the board the tenser his eyes became, concentration spreading over his face like liquid over a blotter. Never lifting his eyes from the board, he wrinkled his brow, scratched his neck, pulled at his nose, thrust out his lower lip, raised his eyebrows in surprise, nibbled on his tongue, and scowled, his face in constant motion, constant flux, floating here and floating there, until, calm at last, its efforts over, he smiled a smile of sly encouragement. And though I knew nothing at all about chess, I could tell by looking at him that the smile was a show of homage to his opponent and that something unexpected had happened, something that spelled his inevitable defeat.

SONYA

1

Boulevards are like people: similar in their youth, they undergo gradual change according to what ferments in them.

There were boulevards where a network of crisscrossed sticks, long and red, set off a pond edged with grease spots, an oily pot filled with water, its green surface skimmed by steam-engine clouds and wrinkled by every passing boat; where, not far off, in a large but very low, roofless, bottomless box of reddish sand, a number of children rummaged about, while bench-bound nannies, governesses, and mothers knitted socks and read books, and a breeze blew leafy arabesques like flickering wallpaper across their faces, laps, and the sand.

There were noisy boulevards where military bands would play and red-lizard trams float to heaven in the shiny brass of the instruments; where passersby, strolling to a minatory march, would fall willy-nilly into step, mortified, as into a pit of shame; where, for want of bench space, folding chairs would be set out, chairs with green metal legs and yellow slatted seats that left a terrace-like pattern on one's coat; and where, toward evening, while the trumpets sang of Faust, the bells of a nearby church struck up their clear, piercing chime, as if to foretoken an impending clap of velvet thunder that would make the waltzing trumpets sound unbearably false.

And there were boulevards that seemed boring at first, but were not, boulevards where the sunflower shells were so thoroughly mixed with the dust-gray sand that they could not be swept away; where the pissoir, in the form of a slightly raised, partially open scroll, gave off such a smell that it made one's eyes smart from a distance; where the evenings brought out painted old women in rags hawking twenty-kopeck love in lifeless, scratchy gramophone-record voices, while the days saw people scurrying past the circus poster of a beauty in tights leaping through a torn hoop, her peach-colored thigh pierced by the nail holding the poster in place; and if anyone did chance to perch on a dusty, empty bench, it was merely to rest his load or else, having gobbled up enough sulfur matches or taken a sufficient swig of acid from the apothecary's phial, to fall on his back and, writhing in pain, have one last look at the watery Moscow sky above him.

It was summer, and examinations were a thing of the past, yet I found it harder and harder to muster enthusiasm at the prospect of entering the university, and I began to feel noticeably more depressed by the idle existence I was leading than by the tensions that had brought it about. Indeed, only once or twice a week, when I happened to have a few rubles at my disposal—the wherewithal for a coachman and a room—only then would I venture out.

Those few rubles—there were never more than forty in any one month—weighed heavily on my mother's existence. For a goodly number of years she had worn one and the same tattered, patched, evil-smelling rag of a dress with a pair of scruffy, down-at-heel shoes that could only have exacerbated the pain in her swollen feet, but whenever she had any money she would hand it over to me with great joy. And I, I would take it from her like a man withdrawing an insignificant sum from his account and making a great display of condescension and nonchalance to attest the magnitude of the balance. We never went outside together. Since I did not particularly hide the shame I felt at seeing her dressed so shabbily (though I did try to hide my shame at her ugly old age), she was aware of it, and the few times she met me in the street she would smile a kind, apologetic sort of smile and look beyond or past me, thereby releasing me from the obligation to greet or approach her.

Only on the days when I happened to have money, and only in the evening—when the gaslamps shone, one on, one off, and the shops were closed, the trams empty—would I venture out of doors. Wearing tight, ribbed slacks which, though out of style, showed off my legs far too well for me to give them up, a cap as broad as a floppy-brimmed woman's hat, a tunic with a high woolen collar that gave me a double chin, and sporting a face powdered like a clown's and eyes coated with vaseline, I would stroll up and down the boulevards and try to catch the eye of every passing woman.

I never, as the saying goes, "undressed them" with my glance, nor did I feel any carnal desire for them. In that feverish state, which might have inspired another, say, to write poetry, I would simply stare into the eyes of all women walking in the other direction and wait for a similarly terrifying, wide-eyed look in response. I never accosted a woman who responded with a smile, because I knew that anyone who smiled at a look like mine could be only a prostitute or a virgin. At that time of night not even the fantasy of physical nudity had as much power to make my throat run dry or start me trembling as had that sinister bloodcurdling, deep-probing, lashing look. It was a hangman's look, a look like the contact of sexual organs. The moment I found it—and sooner or later I always did—I would turn on my heel, catch up with the women who had proffered it, and raise white glove to black visor.

Now it would seem that the look the woman and I had just exchanged—the kind of a look we might have exchanged if, an hour before, the two of us had murdered an infant—it would seem that a look like that said everything there was to say. In fact, however, things were much more complex, and when I went up to the woman and made a verbal overture, the sense of which always seemed to reside in the continuation of a recently interrupted conversation, I felt constrained to go on talking and talking in the hope that the words would cultivate a *cordiality* between us and unite that cordiality with the carnality of our initial signal. As we walked along side by side in the obscurity of the boulevard, hostile, on guard, and yet needing each other in a sense, I would spout sweet nothings to her. The less truthful they were, the more plausible they sounded. And when at last, motivated by the curious conviction that care in pulling the trigger muffles the shot, I proposed—in passing, as it were—that we stop in at a hotel for an hour or so, only to have a chat, of course, and only because the weather that day (depending on the circumstances) was so cold or so stultifying, I could tell by her refusal (which nearly always followed) or, rather, by its tone—to what extent it was emotional, indignant, calm, scornful, fearful, or dubious—whether it made any sense to take the woman by the arm and continue to importune her or whether it would be better to about-face and walk off without saying good-bye.

There were also times when, just as I was catching up with one woman who had hooked and beckoned me with that terrifying look, another, from the crowd moving towards me, would cast a glance that was equally inviting and spine-tingling, and I would stop, paralyzed by indecision and the necessity to make a quick choice. But then, noticing that the second woman had turned her head, I would swing round and follow her, still looking back at the first, who was moving off farther and farther in the opposite direction, and suddenly seeing *her* look back, I would compare the two of them and leave off following the second to run back after the first, who had gone so far by then that I often had trouble finding her, and pushing aside anyone who got in my way, I would race forward in search of her, and the faster I raced and the longer I searched, the more sincerely did I believe that she and none other—the woman who had beckoned to me and then vanished into that cursed crowd—represented a dream of perfection, which, like any dream, I would never be able to catch hold of or find again.

An evening beginning with defeat heralded a series of defeats. Walking the boulevards for three hours after a number of failures—one feeding the next, since with each new rebuff I would lose more of my feverish guile and grow increasingly impatient and coarse, revenging myself on the insults of previous women by insulting their successors. Tired, exhausted from the strain, my shoes white from dust, my throat dry from indignities, I not only lost all semblance of sexual desire but began to feel completely sexless, and yet I would go on roaming the streets, possessed by a bitter perversity, the seering pain of the unjustly rejected suitor holding me back and keeping me from returning home.

I had known the same painful feeling as a child. During my first year at school a new boy had entered our class, a boy I took an immediate liking to, but since, then as now, I was agonizingly bashful about expressing my feelings, I had no idea how to approach him, much less strike up a friendship with him. Then one day at lunch, when the boy was taking out his food and unwrapping a roll, I went up to him and, wishing to win him over with a joke, made believe I wanted to grab his lunch. To my surprise, however, he dodged in fear, blushed in anger, and called me a name. Forcing myself to keep smiling, yet blushing with shame for smiling so pitiably and trying thereby to save face, I made another move in his direction, as though I still wanted to grab his lunch. The boy took a swing at me, then another. He was older and stronger than I was, and he gave me a good licking. Later, sitting in a far-off corner crying and snuffling, my tears were genuinely bitter: not because I had been physically hurt but because I had been beaten on account of a three-kopeck roll that I had grabbed for as a way of offering the gift of my friendship, a part of my soul.

Beaten in this sense, I would wander through the long Moscow nights, and when, as the boulevards emptied of people and the standards I set for the woman of my fancy diminished accordingly, I eventually came upon a pitiable slut agreeable to anything, I would find that, reaching the gates of the hotel in the cold, pink hours of morning I felt totally calm and wanted nothing from her, and if I stayed and booked a room all the same, I did so more out of an odd feeling of obligation to the woman than for my own enjoyment. Though perhaps that is not at all the case, because it was in those moments and those moments alone that the sensuality I believed had guided me through the evening came to the fore at last.

2

It all began in August, when Yag, back from Kazan, came straight to my place from the station and, waking me, tugging at me, making me dress, dragged me along with him. He had an expensive cab waiting downstairs, but since he must have hired it at the station it was not one of the finest. The horse had a doleful look about it and was too small for so high a cab, especially one that ran on automobile tires; moreover, the cab itself, its lacquered mudguards badly chipped and joints lined with rust, listed heavily to my side. Yag was wearing a light gray suit (the sleeves were badly wrinkled, probably from the suitcases) and a white panama hat with a tricolor ribbon, but his face was yellow with red spots like nettle stings under the eyes and railway soot dotted the eyes themselves and their blond eyebrows. Staring at the moist black smuts in the corners of those eyes, I felt an almost pathological urge to dab them away with a handkerchief. But Yag interpreted my stare in his own way, and continually raising his arm so that the crook of his cane kept sliding down his sleeve, continually pulling down the front of his panama, which the wind kept blowing back, he smiled at me with feverish lips.

"Handsome as ever," he shouted at me through the wind, "though I can see in your eyes"—at this point the brim of his panama flew up again—"the immortal misery of the empty pocket." Whereupon he muttered something into the wind, something like "No offense meant," and, wrinkling his forehead and leaning back to get at his pocket, he drew out a roll of hundred-ruble notes, tore one off, crumpled it up, and thrust it into my hand. "Take it, take it, you fool!" he cried, warding off refusal with fury. "It comes from a Russian, doesn't it? Not from one of those Europeans." And all at once he began reminiscing about Kazan and his father, whom he called Papa dear, and suddenly we had no trouble talking: the cab had hit a stretch of asphalt, and we could have been riding on butter had it not been for the clip-clop of the hoofs, which so increased in frequency that the horse seemed constantly on the point of stumbling.

Yet I felt bad. The hundred rubles, which were unexpected and more than welcome, shamed me into accommodating Yag, no matter how I tried to hold out. I listened to his boring story about Papa dear with exaggerated attention and was careful to squeeze into the corner each time the listing cab slid him over in my direction. First resisting, then yielding to necessity, I felt with humiliating clarity that I was losing my independent ironic stance vis-à-vis Yag, the very self he had given the money to. My true self, I knew, lay just beneath the surface, and I would recall it the moment I was free of—no, not the money, I needed that—the moment I was free of Yag's presence. For the time being, however, I could not get away, and using one of his stale jokes as an excuse to laugh so disgustingly hard that I felt like punching my own face in, I unobtrusively stuffed the money into my pocket as if I had just picked it out of his.

We ordered vodka at a tavern-like restaurant with the chauvinist Russian name of The Eagle plastered across its yellow-green signboard in white letters. The vodka was served in a white teapot, and I could not help envying Yag each time I saw him drink from his cup: he would pour the vodka down his throat without swallowing, his face showing no sign of a wrinkle and, in fact, seeming to light up from the inside.

I was different. The moist vodka burn—especially the one immediately after a swallow, when the breath, cooling a fiery mouth and throat, takes on the revolting odor of alcohol—filled me with disgust. I drank vodka because intemperance was considered one of the components of bravado and because I wanted to prove—to whom and for what reason I cannot say—that I had the ability to drink more than anyone else and remain sober longer. And even though I was in a terribly bad way myself and had to command each move I wanted to make and then carry out each command with great concentration, still I felt I had scored a victory when after many teapots Yag took a gulp from his cup and, turning pale, suddenly closed his eyes, propped his head up on his hand, and began breathing so hard his whole body shook. The lights had been turned on by then, and flies were fluttering circles round the bulbs. A contraption of tremulous wooden lyres against a blue net background rent the air with lifeless music.

Late in the evening, just before closing time, we found ourselves in a fashionable café, where, keeping an eye on our all-but-comatose faces in the mirrors, we made our way across the floor as if across a rolling deck, pitching forward and forging ahead when it rose up beneath us and tilting backward and braking when it fell out from under our feet. On our way out Yag bought some homebrew from the doorman, whose combination of majesty and servility called to mind a dignitary in disgrace, and arranged with two of the waitresses to go out for a spin and finish off the evening at their place.

Downstairs, near the dark and noisy alleyway where we had agreed to wait for them, we made our introductions. Their names were Nelly and Kitty, which Yag immediately Russified into Nastyukha and Katyukha. Then, with a couple of paternal pats on the behind, he shooed them up into our carriages, and off we went.

All I caught of Kitty was her small, thin figure and the mouse-tail ringlets of hair she wore glued to her cheeks. I rode with Nelly, and a pleasant, windswept ride it was, too. The rows of streetlamps and even the few passersby seemed motionless until we were almost upon them, at which point they jerked into action and flew by. Nelly was sitting next to me. Her neck showed a distinct curvature, but by smiling and constantly screwing up her eyes she managed at times to turn deformity into a sort of flirtation. And probably because my head was still spinning with vodka, which freed me of the necessity to imagine what the passersby might think of me, I started kissing her. She had the most obnoxious habit of sending a *mmm* through her nose each time I pressed against her cold, wet, tightly shut lips, a *mmm* that rose in pitch until it reached a squeal and she began to push me away.

As soon as we had passed through a dark gateway with the number eight just above it—a figure made up of two flirtatiously open, not quite touching circles that shone kerosene yellow in the glow of an invisible streetlamp—the coachmen jumped down and began haggling sullenly over the higher rate they wanted to squeeze from us. Then Nelly and Kitty took us by the hand, pulled us up a dark stairway, and, after fiddling with the lock for a time, led us into the passageway of a flat obviously not belonging to them. Finally they opened yet another door, and through the dark of the room we saw a pre-morning light shining in the window. The moment they turned the light on, however, night returned.

"Just don't make any noise," Nelly pleaded, putting a manicured but working-class hand to her throat. "No noise, please, gentlemen." Meanwhile, Kitty carefully moved the tiny couch away from the wall and, crossing behind it, spread her red-silk fringed kerchief over the table lamp.

"You haven't a thing to worry about, my sweet," Yag exclaimed in full voice, which made the girls tuck their heads between their shoulders as though he had just given the order to have them flogged. "If your lungs and the couch's springs hold out, there won't be a sound." And Yag threw his head back, smiled, opened his arms to engulf us all.

But just after we were all at last settled on the couch and Yag had taken the first swig of the turbid, swamp-like homebrew, he began to feel sick. All at once his pale face broke out in a sweat and he gave a noisy snort. Then he stood up and, opening his mouth wide, made his way to the window, leaned his chest against the windowsill, and, his back shaking, began to puke. I, too, felt nauseous and kept swallowing and swallowing, but each time my mouth would fill up again. Kitty held her hands modestly over her eyes, but I could see a laughing black eye looking out at me between her fingers. As for Nelly, she kept her eyes on Yag, but the corners of her lips had turned down in disdain and she was shaking her head as if to say her presentiments about us had been fully confirmed.

Yag returned from the window in top form, however, and after wiping his eyes and his mouth he dropped to the couch with a thud, a new idea in mind. "It's time we got cracking," he said, putting his arms around Nelly and trying to press her to him. Each time she pushed back his face with her hand, he would turn, without letting her go, and look over at me, whereupon I would smile back encouragingly, as if cheering him on in some amusing undertaking. Attempting to clasp her to him once and for all, Yag tilted more and more in her direction until one leg, waving in the air in search of support, came in contact with the table and gave it a vigorous kick.

For several seconds after the ensuing racket, or what sounded like a racket to us, we sat as if glued to the spot, straining our ears and breathing deeply. Through the window we could see sparrows perching on the wires like barbs. With great caution I started righting the overturned table, as if the silence with which I picked it up could mitigate the racket it had made when it fell.

"I certainly hope . . ." Yag began, but Nelly, her eyes flashing, cut him short with a Shh!, and Kitty held out her arm and kept it suspended in warning. Sure enough, at that very moment the sound of a door shutting softly came from the passageway. It was followed by the shuffle of feet approaching and finally stopping at our door. Then the handle started moving slowly, terrifyingly, and in the crack I saw a panic-stricken eye staring at me. Suddenly the door flew open and, with scandalous pluck, in stepped a pair of men's pajamas. The pajama top collar was turned up around the head of a charming woman, whose backless, high-heeled red slippers flopped and scraped as she walked.

"Well?" she said, looking at Nelly and Kitty, as if neither Yag nor I were in the room. "A fine pair of lodgers you are, I see! Is this what it's going to be like every night?"

Nelly and Kitty were sitting side by side on the couch. Nelly of the crooked neck gaped at the woman with wide, blinking eyes and a wide-open mouth, while Kitty lowered her head and traced circles on her knees with her fingers, wrinkling her brows and pursing her lips as if about to whistle. It was Yag who saved the day, and not at all because he was drunk; he saved the day because, by pretending to be drunk, he could not be counted among the guilty. Opening his arms so wide that his knees fairly buckled under him, he set off, stomach first, in the direction of the intruder, bleating a drunken song. When he broke off abruptly with a radiant smile, the attractive landlady and I had the following conversation:

SHE: Your friend has a marvelous voice. Though I wonder why he covers his eyes when he sings. Oh, of course! So as not to see me covering my ears.

I: Wit does for a woman's appearance what a man's garment does for her figure: it underscores both her charms and her faults.

SHE: I am afraid that were it not for my garment you would never appreciate my wit.

I: To judge your figure by your wit would be a great pity. I was merely trying to be polite.

SHE: I should greatly prefer your trying to be gallant.

I: Then you have my thanks.

SHE: Your thanks?

I: To be polite is to be sexless, to be gallant is to be erotic.

SHE: In that case may I hasten to assure you I haven't the slightest intention to expect any gallantry from you. Or from your kind, for that matter. A gallant man is one for whom every woman smells like a rose, while for a man like you even a rose seems to smell like a woman. You couldn't even say what a woman is.

I: What a woman is? Of course I could. A woman is like champagne. More intoxicating when cold, more expensive in French trappings.

Flapping her pajama legs and clacking her heels, she came up to me and said softly, "If your definition is correct"—and here she threw a significant sidelong glance in the direction of Nelly and Kitty—"then your wine cellar leaves much to be desired."

Enjoying the discreet rapture of the victor, I held my tongue and dropped my eyes.

"Actually," she added rapidly and in all but a whisper, "we might continue this titillating little talk some other time. My name is Sonya Mintz." And lowering her head as if to peer into my eyes as I bowed respectfully to kiss her outstretched hand, she let out a pleasantly surprised "Oh-ho-ho!" and made a fox face, thereby giving an Oriental slant to her deep blue eyes. Then she straightened up and said to Yag and me, talking this time as if neither Nelly nor Kitty were in the room, that she had nothing against our presence but that she would have to ask us to be a bit more quiet. And so saying she left the room.

The moment the door closed behind her, Yag and I—by tacit agreement, as it were, each feeling exactly what the other felt—began to say our good-byes, Yag rummaging about for his panama and cane, I for my cap. And while Nelly and Kitty accompanied us along the passageway, I felt a combination of disgust and fear at the thought that someone at the other end of the flat might hear an intimate word between one of the girls and me, a word that would bind me to them, and I wanted to get away as soon as possible, to avoid talking to them and touching them, to disassociate myself from them completely. But once down the stairs and out in the courtyard, I felt a sudden stab of pity for the girls, a well-meaning sort of pity, as if they had been deeply and unjustly wronged and I, for one, were to blame.

3

Next morning I woke up with—or rather was awakened by—a feeling of acute anxiety together with what was for me an uncommonly intense awareness of joy, a feeling accompanied by a raging headache, a metallic dryness in the mouth, and a series of needle-like jabs in the heart, all quite usual after vodka. It was still early. Nanny was shuffling along the passageway whispering *pssh pssh pssh,* and the words behind the *pssh pssh,* words she ascribed to the person she was arguing with, finally made her so indignant that just as she reached my door she stopped and cried out, "Well, I never! Not on your life!"

I turned over on my side, curled up into a ball,

and sighed, as if to say, "I'm so depressed," while in fact I felt wonderful, marvelous; I made believe I wanted to go back to sleep, knowing full well that in my state of joyful anxiety it was impossible not only to fall asleep but even to remain in bed. From the kitchen I could hear the dry *chirr* of water from the tap, hear it pass into a resonant rumble and slowly rise in pitch as it filled the pot beneath it. There was something so moving in those sounds that, feeling the need to release my pent-up joy, I lifted myself up—thereby shifting the needle in my heart and sending a dull, venomous pain through my temples—and shouted as loud as I could for Nanny. The tap fell silent immediately, but no shuffle of slippers followed. When Nanny suddenly entered, she might have been walking on a cloud—though I did not need to look at her feet to know for certain why she made no noise.

"What is it, Vadichka?" she asked. "You'll wake the mistress, screaming your lungs out before the sun comes up!" Her tiny sixty-year-old face, the color of an autumn leaf, was solemn and concerned.

"What's the idea, you witch, you!" I cried, without raising my head. "Wearing felt boots in summer!" I could feel the pain between the back of my neck and the pillow start to quiver as the intensity died down.

"It's my legs, my aching legs, Vadichka," she said solicitously, but immediately added a matter-of-fact, "Is that the only reason you called?" And shaking her head reproachfully, her hand over her mouth, she looked down at me with laughing eyes full of affection.

"It is," I said, hoping the soporific calm of my voice would fool her. "The only reason." Then all of a sudden I bounded out of bed in a fury and—doubling over like a murderer ready to pounce, flinging back my arms as if I had daggers in both hands and stamping on the floor with my bare feet to simulate the chase I meant to give the old woman, who was fleeing in terror as it was—bellowed ferociously, "Out! Scat! Shoo! Get away with you!"

But that was not the end of the performance I gave that morning, a performance I imagined to be taking place before the deep blue eyes of Sonya Mintz. Everything I did that morning I did differently: I did it as if Sonya were watching my every move and enjoying it all immensely. (I attributed her enthusiasm to the changes I had inaugurated, to what made that day different from the daily routine.) Thus, taking a clean shirt from the wardrobe, the only silk shirt I owned, I threw it to the floor after a cursory inspection—the shoulder seam had begun to come undone—and trampled it underfoot as if I had a dozen of them. When I cut myself shaving, I continued to scrape the razor over the gash, pretending I could not feel it in the least. Changing my underwear, I thrust out my chest and sucked in my stomach until I was ready to burst, as if that magnificent physique were really mine. After a sip of coffee I pushed my cup aside like a spoiled brat, though the coffee was perfectly good and I wanted to go on drinking it. Like it or not, I had that morning stumbled on the amazing yet absolutely incontrovertible fact that as I was, in reality, I could never be admired, much less loved, by someone I myself loved.

It was about eleven when, after a precautionary dip into my pocket for Yag's hundred-ruble note, I went outside. There was no sun, and the sky was low and a soft white, but one look at it and my eyes started tearing. It was stuffy and humid. My anxiety grew more and more acute. It had taken over all my senses and even made itself painfully felt in the upper regions of my stomach. To get to the florist's I had to pass a fashionable and expensive hotel, and for some reason I decided to stop off there. I gave the revolving door a push and watched the building next door jerk into motion in the glass. Then I stepped inside and walked across the lobby. The café was so deserted, the odors of cigar smoke, napkin starch, honey, armchair leather, and coffee so permeated with the aggravations of travel that I felt I could not stand another minute of it, and, making believe I was looking for someone, quickly slipped outside again.

I cannot tell quite when I hit upon the idea of sending Sonya flowers; I only know that the plan grew in importance the closer I came to the florist's. At first I thought of sending her a ten-ruble basket, then a twenty-ruble basket, then a forty-ruble basket, and, since Sonya's joy and amazement kept growing with the size of the bouquet, by the time I reached the shop I had come to the conclusion that the only thing to do was to spend the entire hundred rubles on flowers. I walked past a window of wrinkled flower faces spotted with tears of water trickling down the inside of the glass, and crossed the threshold. But no sooner had I inhaled the damp, fragrant half-light of my surroundings than I shut my eyes—mentally, at least—in terrible shock: there, in the shop, stood Sonya herself!

I was wearing an old school cap with a faded band and cracked visor, the same musty tunic I had worn the day before, and a pair of baggy, threadbare trousers; my knees were trembling violently; I had broken out into the rank sweat of a fire victim. There was no way out, however: there in front of me was a saleswoman asking whether Monsieur would like a basket or a bouquet, having pointed out by then not only ten or so different kinds of flowers I may have known by sight but was unable, for the most part, to identify by name, but also enumerated a good ten kinds I had never seen before.

At that point Sonya turned round and walked straight at me with a tranquil smile. She was wearing a gray suit, its lapel bunched up by a posy of clumsily attached artificial violets, and flat-heeled shoes, which pointed outward in an unfeminine way when she walked. Not until she had sailed past on her way to the cash-desk behind me did I realize that she was not smiling at me, or at anything she had seen, for that matter, but at her own thoughts. And suddenly behind my back I heard that peculiar, slightly cracked voice of hers, which I had tried all morning to conjure up, say to the saleswoman opening the door for her, "Please have the flowers delivered immediately or the gentleman may go out and I should be very displeased. Thank you." And off she went.

Even as I looked for a spot on the way home to toss the few carnations I had bought for the sake of propriety, I knew for certain I was finished with Sonya. Oh, I was perfectly aware that there had never been anything between us to begin with, that it had all been *in me* rather than *with her,* that Sonya could not possibly have known how I felt, and that the onus was on me to *win her over,* to communicate my feelings to her and induce her to share them. In fact, it was the very thought of having to win Sonya's love—the necessity to state my case and make my feelings persuasive to a person who did not yet trust me and was therefore alien to me—that made it absolutely plain I was finished with her. Perhaps all courtship requires a modicum of odious prevarication, a smile-sweetened wait-and-see kind of hostility. But the outrage I so keenly felt at the thought of it distanced me from the living Sonya the moment I started thinking of the necessity to *win her over.* I could not quite explain the feeling, but it was the same bitter outrage that would have kept me from even trying to convince the woman I loved of my innocence had she suspected me, an honest man, of theft, whereas nothing of the sort would have held me back had I been indifferent to the woman in question. In these short minutes I realized for the first time in my life and on the basis of my own experience that even the lowest of the low have feelings of unrelenting pride, feelings demanding absolute reciprocity and preferring the pain of bitter solitude to the joy of a success gained at the humiliating expense of reason.

And who was the gentleman she sent the flowers to? I wondered. Suddenly I felt so exhausted that I all but stretched out on the spot, on the stairs. Gentleman. Gen-tle-man. What did it mean, anyway? "Master"—now that was clear and convincing, but "gentleman" was neither here nor there. I unlocked the door, walked down the passageway of our wretched little flat, and, intending to stretch out immediately on my couch, went into my room. Although the room had been made up, it gave off a Summery atmosphere of dust and light and misery. But on the desk lay a bulky tissue-paper package with pins running up the seam. It was Sonya's flowers with a note asking me to see her that very evening.

4

By evening the rain had stopped, but the streets were still wet and streetlamps shone up from what looked like dark lakes. Although the giant candelabra flanking the granite statue of Gogol were buzzing softly, the milky bulbs in wire netting suspended from the top of the cast-iron masts sent down but little light: a handful of golden coins blinking randomly among piles of black, wet leaves. As we passed, a raindrop falling from the sharp nose, the sharp stone nose, latched on to the beam of the lamp, flashed blue for an instant, and then went out.

"Did you see it?" asked Sonya.

Yes. Of course I'd seen it.

Slowly, silently we moved on, turning down the

next small street. In the damp still of the air we could hear a piano playing, but, as so often happens in the street, part of the sound had dispersed and we caught only the more resonant part, which attacked the stones so piercingly that someone up in the room seemed to be pounding a bell with a hammer. Not until we were directly under the window did all the sounds come together: it was a tango.

"Do you like it?" asked Sonya. "It's Spanish."

No, I said, more or less at random. I preferred the Russian style.

"Why?"

I didn't know why.

"The Spaniard always sings about tormented passion, the Russian about passionate torment. Maybe that's why."

Yes. Of course. "Yes, that's it . . . Sonya," I said, thus overcoming the bittersweet obstacle of her gentle name.

We turned another corner. It was even darker there. Only one window, on the ground floor, shone brightly, casting a square of light on the wet, round cobblestones below: a tray with apricots. Suddenly Sonya let out an "Oh!" and dropped her handbag. I quickly bent down, picked it up, and pulled out my handkerchief to wipe it off. Paying no attention to what I was doing, Sonya gazed intently into my eyes. She put out her hand, removed the cap from my head, and, nestling it in her arms as if it were a tiny kitten, started stroking it with the tips of her fingers. Perhaps because of that or perhaps because she had not yet lowered her eyes from mine, I took a step in her direction (her bag in one hand, my handkerchief in the other) and, afraid of falling into a swoon, put my arms around her. "You have my permission," said her languidly half-shut eyes.

I leaned over and brushed my lips against hers. Such was perhaps the inhuman chastity with which the dry, sexless, yet awe-inspiring martyrs of long ago would brush their lips against the icons in their sweet and painful, their joyous zeal to renounce heart, soul, and life.

"Dearest," said Sonya plaintively, first withdrawing her lips, then proffering them again, "dearest child. Darling. You do love me, don't you? Come, say it."

Hard as I sought the words, the words I was now called upon to pronounce, the wondrous, magic words of love, I could not find them in me. My experience in matters of love seemed to have convinced me that no one could talk eloquently of love unless his love was only a memory, that no one could talk persuasively of love unless his sensuality was aroused, and no one whose heart was actually in the throes of love could say a word.

5

Two weeks went by, during which time my feeling of joy grew anxious and feverish, tainted as it was by the lacerated torment that comes with joy amassed in too dense a fashion, within a period of days, instead of flowing through the years in a free and even stream.

Everything in me had split in two.

My sense of time was split. Morning would be followed by a rendezvous with Sonya, then lunch in a restaurant and a drive into the countryside, and soon it was night. The whole day raced past like a falling stone. But all I had to do was look back on any one of those days in my mind's eye and suddenly they seemed months, so heavily charged were they with impressions.

My sense of attraction to Sonya was split. Since whenever we were together I felt a constant and intense desire to please her and a constant and violent fear that she would be bored with me, I was always in such torment by nightfall that I would heave a sigh of relief when Sonya turned and passed through the gate and I was left alone. Yet no sooner did I reach home than I again began to feel that itch, that longing for Sonya, and, neither eating nor sleeping, grew more feverish the closer the moment of our rendezvous approached, until, a half hour or so before we were to meet, I was in agony once again at the prospect of making myself interesting, and felt relieved when I was left alone.

My sense of inner self was split. My intimacy with Sonya had not gone beyond the kissing stage, and the only feeling our kisses aroused in me was the tearful tenderness of train departures and prolonged, perhaps permanent, absence. Kisses like those have too much of an effect on the heart to affect the body. And since they provided the base, as it were, for our relations, they forced me into the role of the dreamy, even callow youth. Sonya seemed to revive feelings long since dead in me, feelings younger than myself, of a purity and naïveté that belied my foul experience. Within a few days of behaving thus with Sonya I came to believe that it was how I actually was, that I could never be any different. Yet only two or three days later, when I ran into Takadzhiev—who had approved of, even delighted in, the "personal" view of women I had expounded upon at school, and who had seen me several times in Sonya's company—my conscience started acting up and I felt an uncontrollable urge to justify my actions to him. I felt what a thief must feel when, abandoning his trade thanks to a hard-working family that has given him a roof over his head, he meets an old comrade in crime and suffers pangs of conscience over having failed to rob his benefactors. Once our cordial salutatory obscenities were over, I explained to him that the frequency of my trysts with *that woman* (which was how I referred to Sonya) was due exclusively to my erotic appetite, which she was extraordinarily skillful in exciting and satisfying. The split, the duality within me, lay not so much in the lie pronounced by my lips as in the truth revealed in my insolent, swaggering essence.

My sense of the people around me had also split in two. As a result of my feelings for Sonya I became—in comparison with what I had been—extremely kind. I was generous in giving alms (and more generous when alone than when in Sonya's presence), made Nanny laugh all the time, and once, on my way home late one night, stood up for a prostitute whom I had seen insulted by a passerby. But my new attitude towards people, my joyful longing to embrace the world, as it were, would immediately turn into a longing to destroy that world the moment anyone happened to come between Sonya and me, no matter how indirectly.

Within a week most of the hundred rubles Yag had given me were gone. The few left were not enough to enable me to keep my appointment with Sonya, because on that day we had agreed to have an early lunch and drive to Sokolniki for the rest of the day.

Having gulped down my morning coffee in disgust and in that state of agitation which often leads to searing stomach pains—I was racked by the thought of what was to come and the problem of spending moneyless days with Sonya—I went into my mother's room and told her I needed money. She was sitting by the window in her armchair, looking particularly yellow. There was a tangle of multicolored thread in the embroidery frame in her lap, but her hands lay idle and her faded eyes stared off into a corner, heavy and listless.

"I need money," I repeated, opening my fingers wide like a duck's foot, because she had not moved, "and I need it now."

After a visible effort Mother managed to raise her arms a little, but almost immediately dropped them again in docile desperation.

"Well, if you haven't got any," I said, "then give me your brooch. I can pawn it." (The brooch was an all but sacred object for her, the only keepsake she had from my father.)

Still not responding, still staring straight ahead of her, she rummaged in the old-fashioned bodice of her blouse with a quivering hand and withdrew a canary-yellow pawn ticket.

"But I need money!" I whined, in despair at the idea of Sonya waiting for me in vain. "I need money, and I'll sell the flat, I'll break the law to get it." I ran through the tiny room and out into the passageway—though I would have been hard put to say why—where I bumped into Nanny, who had been listening at the door.

"Just what I needed, you old witch," I said, brutally shoving her out of the way.

But Nanny, trembling with defiance, seized my hand as if to kiss it, and, holding me back, looking me up and down with the prayerful insistence she usually reserved for icons, whispered, "Don't hurt the mistress, Vadya. It'll be the death of her, Vadya. She's halfway there as it is. Today's the anniversary of your father's death." No longer able to look me in the eye, she stared at my chin. Then, after wiping her button-like nose with her hand, she added, embarrassed as only an old woman can be, "If . . . if it's money you need, take mine, will you? Say you will, please! For the love of Christ, say yes! You're not angry, are you?" And off to the kitchen she shuffled, to return a moment later with a bundle of ten-ruble bills. I knew she had accumulated that money through years of toil and was saving it for the almshouse to assure herself a corner in her old age when she could no longer work for a living—yet still I took it. As she handed me the money, she sniffled and blinked, ashamed of showing me her joyful tears of love and self-abnegation.

Two days later Sonya and I were riding along one of the boulevards on our way to the country when Sonya realized she needed to phone home. She stopped the driver—we happened to be in a square not far from my house—and asked me to wait for her. I jumped out of the cab and began walking up and down to pass the time when, almost at the corner, I felt someone touch my hand. I turned. It was Mother. Hatless, her wispy gray hair badly ruffled, she was wearing Nanny's old quilted jacket and carrying a string bag of groceries.

"I've managed to come up with a little money," she said, stroking my shoulder timidly, beseechingly. "If you like, I can . . ."

"Go away, go away!" I said, interrupting her, terribly apprehensive that Sonya would come out, see us, and guess that that horrid old woman was my mother. "What are you waiting for, Madame?" Unable to raise my voice in the street, I tried to make my point by calling her "Madame." "Be on your way, do you hear?"

But the moment I returned to the cab and helped Sonya up to her place—she had just then made her appearance—I felt such a surge of happiness at the sight of her blue eyes, squinting as they were from the sun reflected in the lacquered mudguards, that I could gaze with equanimity on the gray head, quilted jacket, and swollen legs hobbling along the other side of the street in worn-down boots.

Next morning, on my way to have a wash, I ran into Mother in the hall. Feeling pity for her, yet uncertain of what to say about what had happened, I stopped and ran my hand over her flaccid cheek. To my surprise she neither smiled nor showed any sign of joy; instead, her face turned into a pitiful mass of wrinkles, and tears, boiling hot (or so it seemed to me at the time), began flowing down her cheeks. She seemed to be trying to say something and might well have succeeded had I not decided that everything had now been smoothed over and, not wishing to be late, quickly moved on.

Such was my attitude toward the outside world, such was its duality: on the one hand, a desire, only natural in one who loves, to embrace the world, make others happy, love them himself; on the other, the shameless expropriation of an old woman's hard-earned kopecks coupled with boundless filial cruelty. What made it rather more curious was that I saw no contradiction whatever between my cruel lack of scruples and the rushes of love I felt for the entire universe. It was as if experiencing these good, kind feelings, so alien to my character, had in fact given me the strength to commit acts of cruelty which in the absence of such feelings I would never have believed myself capable of.

But of all the splits in my character the one most clearly drawn and keenly felt was the split between spirit and flesh.

6

Late one night, having seen Sonya home and started back to my own flat, I came to a deserted square, all the more desolate for being brightly lit, and crossed it in such a way as to avoid a group of prostitutes sitting on a bench outside its small tram station. As usual, the provocations and propositions they shouted out to me deeply wounded my male pride, which saw them as negating the possibility of receiving gratis from other women what these women offered me for money.

Though the Tverskaya Street prostitutes were sometimes a good deal more attractive than the women I found and followed along the boulevards, though going with a prostitute would not have been a bit more expensive nor the danger of infection any greater, and though by choosing a prostitute I would have saved hours of wandering, searching, and ignominious defeats, still I never had anything to do with them.

I had nothing to do with prostitutes because I had no interest in intercourse legitimized by verbal agreement; what I was after was the cruel and covert battle, the gains and final victory, which I saw as a victory of my self, my body, something mine and mine alone, not like a handful of rubles that might belong to anyone. I had nothing to do with prostitutes because by accepting payment in advance a prostitute was under an *obligation* to bestow her favors, she did so under duress—perhaps (as I pictured it) gritting her teeth the while and desiring nothing more than to get it over with as soon as possible and leave. By dint of such hostile impatience my bed companion would be more of a bored onlooker than a hot-blooded partner, any arousal I might feel was in a sense a mirror image of the feeling the woman had for me.

Before I was halfway down the short boulevard, I heard small pattering steps and heavy breathing coming from behind. "Whew! I never thought I'd make it," said a voice repugnantly, professionally playful. I turned to see the yellow light of the square streaming into the cave of the boulevard and a woman running toward me in that light. I stepped aside, but she took a sudden swerve in my direction, rammed into me, and threw her arms around my neck. Her warm, clinging body produced an immediate reaction in my nether regions; her lips—making contact, pressing, opening, and releasing a cold, wet, wriggling tongue into my mouth—confirmed and intensified it. As befits such a moment, I experienced the earth falling out from under me, leaving behind only the tiny piece I was standing on, and, as much as to keep myself from being hurled into the void as for any other reason, I threw my arms around her, too. The rest was terribly simple.

First the cab, which both jolted along and seemed stationary, because I could not help seeing a patch of starry sky while tearing at the girl's lips in blissful savagery; then the gate, a solid wood affair with a small door that opened like the door of a cuckoo clock, and, off to one side, a gold boot hanging from the end of a poker that stuck out from the house; then the corridor, the wood framework of the walls peeking through the peeling plaster and the deep, dust-filled hollows made by the nails in the oilcloth-covered padding that lined the door; then the stagnant, sweltering air of the tiny room; the kerosene lamp, and, on the black ceiling above it, a splash of light so intense it seemed to have come from the sun through a magnifying glass; the multicolored patchwork quilt, damp and heavy enough to have been stuffed with sand; the girl's breast, flopping to one side, with its flabby brown nipple and white pimples round about; and, finally, when all was said and done, the certainty (so often experienced, yet always new) that female charms, the kind that inflame the senses, are no more than kitchen smells: they tease you when you're hungry and disgust you when you've had your fill.

It was morning by the time I left. The transparent heat issuing from the chimney next door had set a patch of the sky aquiver. Although it was light, the sun was not out. The streets were empty, there was no sound of trams. The only soul about was the local watchman, who—gray beard, schoolboy belt, green cap-band and all—was engaged in sweeping the boulevard. Stirring up heavy clouds of dust that immediately settled again, he slowly made his way in my direction like a pair of dividers, he himself being the fixed arm and his broom, on its extra long stick, the other, tracing semi-circles between the stretches of grass. The broom's sturdy twigs left endless rows of scratches in the sand.

Walking along, I felt wonderful, pure, as if my insides had just been given a good wash. The golden needles on the black and otherwise uninteresting clock in the pink monastery tower told me that in one minute it would be a quarter past five, and when, after crossing the square, I looked up at a similar black clock there, its golden needles told me it was a quarter past five on the dot. At that very moment I heard some tinny, bitty sounds such as might have been made by a chicken strolling across a harp.

Seven hours later I was due to meet Sonya again, and the joy and impatience I suddenly felt at the prospect of seeing her took such strong hold of me that I knew I would never be able to fall asleep. "Betrayal—that's what it is," I said to myself, thinking back to the night before. Yet no matter how sincerely I tried to fix that perfidious label to the feelings I had experienced, it kept coming off, peeling off, falling off. It refused to stick. Then what was it? For if what I had done could not be called treason, then my spiritual essence had no responsibility whatever for the sensual in me; my sensuality, as unsavory as it might be, could not besmirch my spirituality; my sensuality was open to all women, my spirituality to Sonya alone; and sensuality and spirituality were for some reason completely separate in me.

Although I knew or at least felt that I had hit upon a kind of truth, deep down I was tormented by a new image I could not put aside, the image of a woman like Sonya finding herself in my situation and doing something similar to what I had done, going through what I had gone through that night. Of course, I both felt—no, knew—that it was impossible, that such a thing could never have happened or ever happen to Sonya, but the very fact that it was so impossible made it amply clear that in her, as in all women, sensuality was able and even bound to sully spirituality, that feminine spirituality was the true culprit in any felony feminine sensuality might commit. The result was that in her, Sonya, as in all women, the spiritual and the sensual had merged, and that to split them, to make them as separate as they were in me, was tantamount to splitting life itself.

Not that I pictured Sonya herself in such a situation. No, it was rather a girl or woman from a family more or less like mine and burning, like me, with a prodigious, unprecedented passion. I saw her returning home alone in the dark of night, accosted by a boulevard dandy, someone she had never seen before and could hardly see then, at least not well enough to tell whether he was young or old and ugly. Then I saw him grabbing hold of her, pressing her to him, kissing her vilely; I saw her yielding, consenting, going home with him, but, most important, leaving the morning after, without so much as a glance at the man she had spent the night with, and returning home feeling completely unsullied and, even worse, looking forward to a chaste rendezvous with the man she loves. There is only one word for a woman like that, and that word is harlot. Suddenly I saw how strange it all was: I saw that if a man does what he does he is a man, and if a woman does what he does she is a harlot. In other words, I saw that *the split between spirituality and sensuality in the male is a sign of virility while the same split in the female is a sign of harlotry.*

Immediately I applied this unexpected epiphany to my own situation. Here I was, Vadim Maslennikov, prospective lawyer and, or so everyone around me seemed to think, prospectively useful and honorable member of society. Yet no matter where I was—on a tram, in a café, at the theater, in a restaurant, in the street, anywhere and everywhere—I had only to glance at a woman's figure, not her face but the seductive fullness or delicacy of her thighs, to picture myself dragging her to a bed, a bench, even a gateway, without so much as a word of introduction. Yes, that is exactly what I would have done had the woman allowed it. And this split between the spiritual and sensual, the reason I felt no moral obstacles in the way of satisfying my instinct, was also the main reason my friends thought me dashing and intrepid. But what if the spiritual and sensual were one? Wouldn't I then fall head over heels in love with every woman who attracted me sexually, and wouldn't my friends mock me continually, call me a petticoat or a lovesick maiden or something of the sort to express their youthful disdain for the femininity of my behavior? In other words, this disassociation between spirit and sex was perceived by my peers as a sign of masculinity, virility.

Now let us suppose that I were a schoolgirl instead of a schoolboy. Let us suppose that I had only to glance at a man—in that same café or tram or theater or street, anywhere and everywhere, not even seeing his face perhaps—to be aroused by the musculature of his thighs and (feeling no moral obstacles in the way of satisfying my instinct) to go up to him smiling and without a word and allow him to drag me off to a bed, a bench, or even a gateway. What impression would my actions make on my peers, the girls I went to school with, or even the men I happened to know? Would they perceive and interpret them as the expression of a dashing, intrepid character? The very thought was absurd. There could be no doubt that I would be publicly stigmatized as a harlot—not a prostitute, who is the victim of circumstances or material deprivation and may therefore be exonerated—but as a common harlot who indulges openly in her basest instincts, which is to say, someone utterly beyond exoneration. And so it is both valid and just that the split between spirituality and sensuality in the male is a sign of virility and the same split in the female a sign of harlotry. And if all womankind banded together and took the male path, the world would turn into one huge brothel.

7

To a man in love, all women are merely women except the woman he loves, who thereby becomes a *person;* to a woman in love, all men are merely men except the man she loves, who thereby becomes a *man.* Such was the unhappy truth I came to accept the further my relationship with Sonya developed. Yet neither on that day nor on any of the following did I talk over my thoughts with her. If I was reluctant to give a true account of myself to my pre-Sonya acquaintances for fear of belying the layer of rodomontade I felt obliged to show the public, I could not be sincere with Sonya without mutilating the image of the dreamy youth she wished to see in me.

The reason I found it impossible to discuss my true feelings with friends was that I wanted more than anything to appear a hero to them, and that I realized that what made a hero heroic was a cheerful, happy-go-lucky front. The moment I made the accounts of what I had been through the least bit profound or thought-provoking, the acts I so boasted of would become cruel and repugnant, completely unjustifiable.

Sonya was the first person with whom I could shed the burden of false merriment and high spirits. For her I was just a sweet little boy, a dreamer. Yet it was this very state of affairs, at first glance so conducive to openness on my part, that stopped me in my tracks the time I tried to tell Sonya the story of my life. All at once, in the midst of my first gush of sincerity, I felt I should not, could not, would not be frank with her. How could I, her dreamy little boy, tell her about infecting Zinochka, about shooing away my mother lest she, Sonya, catch sight of her, about squandering my old nanny's money on expensive coachmen and ice cream for Sonya? How could I tell her all that when even my attempts to talk of deeds that showed only the noble side of my character ended in failure? To begin with, I had never done any good deeds; besides, even if I had simply fabricated a few, I would not have enjoyed going on about them; finally, and most important, tales of good deeds would not have brought us closer together spiritually—the main reason for my sincerity in the first place.

The matter never stopped tormenting me, not so much because I felt doomed to spiritual solitude—which I took too much for granted to notice—as because I was plagued by an acute paucity of conversation topics likely to further the growth of intimacy and love. I knew that love is a feeling that must constantly grow and develop, and that to do so it needs to be helped along; it is like a child's hoop, which, the moment it loses its momentum and starts to slow down, is in danger of toppling over. I knew that lovers who are prevented, by hostile people or circumstances, from meeting frequently and for extended periods of time are happy lovers. Seeing Sonya every day, spending many long hours with her, I did my utmost to keep her entertained, but the words I chose did not appear to further the growth of our love or bring us closer spiritually; they made time pass but put it to no use. The result was a series of empty moments that weighed especially heavy whenever we sat down on a bench alone, for then, terrified at the thought that Sonya would notice or at least sense my painful exertions, I would fill the ever increasing gaps between faltering words with compulsive kisses.

So it was that kisses came to replace words in the role of bringing us together, and, much like words, they grew more and more frank the closer we came to know each other. Kissing Sonya, I experienced too pure a form of adoration, I was too deeply moved—she loved me!—to feel desire, and I could not help comparing the relations I had had with the women of the boulevards and the relation I now had with Sonya: where formerly I had felt only desire, feigning love for the women's sake, now I felt only love, feigning desire for Sonya's sake. When at last our kisses exhausted the possibilities for bringing us together and led me to the final, forbidden frontier of physical intimacy—which I had only to cross, or so it seemed to me then, to achieve the greatest degree of spiritual intimacy vouchsafed to man on earth—I resolved to proceed, and asked Yag to lend me his room for a few hours so I could be alone with her there.

The night I reached the decision—I told her at the gate that the next day we would pay a visit to Yag and then stay on by ourselves, there was nothing wrong in it, Yag was a fine fellow and my best and most devoted friend—that night, even though Sonya responded to my assurances with nothing more than the usual "Oh-ho-ho!" cum fox face and Oriental squint, that night, while walking home, what I looked forward to most was not the pleasures of the flesh but the complete and utter spiritual possession that physical intimacy ensured.

8

The broad, white staircase spiraled upward in semi-circles to a skylight roof. We climbed in a humiliating, business-like silence. Yag led us to his quarters through a large, resonant room in which chairs, piano, and chandelier lay dormant under white dust covers. It was still light out, but Yag's room, which was at an angle to the setting sun, enjoyed no more than the twilight glow that outlined in apricot the chubby balusters showing through the open balcony door.

"No," said Sonya when Yag rushed behind a raspberry-velvet armchair rubbed black in the creases and seized it with such determination that he seemed intent on bowling her over. "No," she said, "let's sit out there." She nodded in the direction of the balcony. "It's so marvelous. We can, can't we?"

By the time she finished her question, Yag had picked up the small round lace-covered table—it was crowded with biscuits, a crystal carafe of green liqueur, and tiny red glasses that looked like overturned fezes, and was moving it outside. "Of course we can, Sofya Petrovna," he said, turning back to her with the table still in his hands and then even putting it down to spread his arms solicitously.

The setting sun, round and fat like the yoke of a raw egg and, though seemingly hooked to the roof, visible in its entirety, gave the faces on the balcony a peony-red tinge.

"May I have the honor of serving you, Sofya Petrovna?" asked Yag, having shown the two of us to our seats. "The liqueur is a minor miracle." He filled the glasses, steadying his elbow with the other hand. "You know, I'd no idea you were even seeing each other, you and Vadim, and now it turns out you're great friends. Do try some." Then, in response to Sonya's nod of gratitude, he himself sat down on the edge of his chair, posing the carafe on one knee and holding it there by the neck like a violinist waiting out a rest.

Sonya, red glass setting off red face, smiled by way of encouragement. "Go on," her lowered eyes seemed to say, "go on. Tell me more."

"After all, Sonya Petrovna," Yag continued, looking directly at her smile, "the night we met, you, to put it mildly, chucked us out on our ears. Not that you weren't right to do so, I might add. But . . . *I* wouldn't have had the nerve to raise my hat to you, to say nothing of . . ."

"To say nothing of what?" Sonya asked, smiling at her glass.

"Why, of this." And Yag made believe he was trying to weigh something by tossing it in the air and catching it in his hand. "What I mean is, I don't know how Vadim managed it, whether he phoned you or dropped you a note. All I know is that after a night like that I wouldn't have dared."

Without removing the glass from her lips, Sonya uttered a dissenting *hmmm* that sounded like a throat being cleared, then flung her hands in the air, and, the glass still between her lips, leaned down over the table and set it down without spilling a drop.

"You've got it all wrong," she said, laughing, her lips still wet. "Whatever gave you that idea? I'm the one who sent the note and the flowers. The very next morning. That's all there is to it."

"Flowers?"

"Uh-huh."

"To him?" Yag asked, disengaging the thumb from his fist and aiming it straight at me.

"To him?" Sonya repeated, imitating him but looking beyond him into my eyes. It's love, the penetrating glance on her smiling face (the kind of look one uses to frighten a baby) seemed to say, love that made me do then what I tell now and love that makes me tell now what I did then.

For a while Yag sat in silence, looking now at me (I looked back with a happy, silly smile), now at Sonya. But gradually his watery eyes—first wide-open from Sonya's confession, then distant from the internal workings of his mind—grew wily.

"May I be so bold, Sofya Petrovna," he said, picking up his glass and taking a sip of the liqueur, then swirling it around with his jaws as if it were a mouth wash, "may I be so bold as to remind you of what you said about some flowers and a note and such? Now tell me, the address, the address you sent them to—how did you come by that? Or did you know it beforehand? You say you did not?" Try as he might he could not translate Sonya's smile into words. "Well then, how did you come by it?"

"It couldn't have been simpler," said Sonya. "Just let me speak. I didn't know a thing about you or Vadim, not a thing. Here's how I came by my information. Early the next morning I called Nelly in, gave her a good talking to and warned her the next time they got involved in such scandalous goings on, the very next time, I would send them packing then and there. How could they, I mean, really, how dared they bring who? strange men! where? to my flat! and when? at night! Well? What am I to make of that? I ask you, what am I to make of that? How can I be sure they weren't crooks? What am I saying? Of course they were crooks. And why are you so sure? Do you know them? Tell me what you know about them."

"I'm sorry, Sofya Petrovna," Yag interrupted, "but your Nastyukha, I mean Nelly, knew neither our names nor our addresses."

"You're right about the addresses," Sonya nodded, "but she did know that the one in the student's tunic was Vadim and the one in the suit Yag. Besides, last winter when she was working for the Muirs, she would see the two of you all the time. You always wore—as she put it—the 'weirdest-looking' uniform: just like a university student's, but with silver buttons instead of gold and without eagles. Even though she didn't know anything else about you, she had given me all I needed. First, I knew the name of the one I was interested in: Vadim. Second, I happened to be familiar with the uniform: the son of a cousin of mine goes to the school where it is worn. Third, I could be certain that if someone had been going about in a school uniform last winter and now wore the tunic of a university student, he had finished school in the spring. I looked up the address of the school and took a cab there. The only one in at the time was the porter, who, after we'd come to know each other a little, went and got me the spring list. I was in luck: of the eighteen names there was only one Vadim. And after I had his surname, the porter immediately provided his address."

"Good for you!" Yag cried out in admiration, whereupon, as if to release him from the obligation of praising her, she put her wrist up to her ear, listened for a moment, then glanced at her watch. Yag, seizing the moment, sent me an urgent eye message to the effect that his departure was imminent.

Evening had fallen and the wind was blowing by the time Yag left. An arc of dust flew up from the street corner, and when—having swept by like a short-lived hurricane, flapping up a tablecloth and eliciting some grimaces from tightly shut eyes—it moved on and vanished, all it left behind was a gritty sugar-like residue in the teeth and an autumn leaf in the form of a banana-colored butterfly fluttering down from what seemed to be the roof, down and down in the air's sudden hush, until at last, just above the table, it did a leisurely somersault into one of the red glasses—a goose feather in a sandbox.

All at once I was sorry Yag had gone, and with him the gratifying wonder of the outsider at my happiness. It was as if my happiness were a new suit that had lost part of its charm from not being worn in public.

Sonya rose, crossed the balcony, and sat down next to me. "Ugh, what an ogre!" she said, wrinkling her face into a mischievous little frown, the frown representing me, and the mischievous look, her response. And fearfully, like a child teasing a dog, she stretched out her index finger and began tracing tiny up-and-down furrows along my lips, making them smack in such a funny way that I soon burst out laughing. "That's how I'll always know," said Sonya. "I'll always know what your feelings are by whether you burst out laughing or push my hand away." She paused, then added, "You see how silly we women are? The effect we produce when we put our observations into words is dearer to us than the use we could make of those observations if we kept them to ourselves."

Darkness had come on quickly, bringing a strong wind and a feeling of apprehension. Only where the sun had gone down, over the black roof of the house, was a narrow tangerine strip still visible. But immediately above it the sky was black, and the clouds, like streams of ink poured into water, scudded in the wind so quickly that when I tilted my head upward, both the balcony and house lurched forward noiselessly, threatening to overrun the city. The leaves on the corner trees whispered sea-like until, just as the moist sound reached its climax, there was a sharp crack up in the branches and all at once a nearby window shattered, crashing resonantly in the roadway after a moment's silence.

"Ugh!" said Sonya. "What an awful place. Let's go in."

After the balcony Yag's room was quiet and as stuffy as if heated. The white tablecloth waved out of the darkness through the closed balcony doors like a farewell handkerchief at a station. Keeping hold of Sonya with one hand, I felt along the crinkly, rustling wallpaper with the other in search of the light switch, but Sonya's hand gently pulled it back. Then, putting both my arms around her, pulling her against me, and clumsily stepping on her toes, I inched her backwards in the direction of a column which loomed white in the dark and which, as I recalled, concealed the bed.

But as I advanced, clutching Sonya to my breast, I foresaw—despite all I did to arouse the male, the animal in me, the demonic energy I so urgently needed—I foresaw, in deep despair and with terrifying clarity, my impending and ineluctable disgrace. For even here in Yag's room, even at the crucial moment, Sonya's presence and Sonya's kisses made me too sensitive to be sensual as well. "What shall I do? What can I do?", I wondered in agony. I knew only too well that Sonya was a woman who had to be taken spontaneously, at one go, not so much because she would offer resistance as because if I dared kindle my temporarily ailing sensuality by means of a long and drawn out process of strokes and palpitations, I would perhaps save my male pride, but I would destroy once and for all the beauty of our relationship.

Even as we reached the column, I kept thinking "What shall I do? What can I do?", desperately certain I was about to bring disgrace upon myself—a disgrace I could never survive—and desperately aware it was the anticipation of disgrace that was robbing me of my last chance to arouse myself and ward it off. And not until the last moment, the moment we tumbled into the black abyss of the vulgarly creaking spring bed, did I come up with a way out. Suddenly I started to moan and, tearing at my tight cloth collar, as I had seen actors do on stage, I said in a rasping voice, "I think I'm going to faint, Sonya. Water!"

9

Moscow, September 1916

Dearest, darling Vadim,

Sad and painful as it is for me to accept it, this is the last letter I shall ever write to you. Ever since that evening (you know the one I mean), things have been strained between us, and once a relationship veers off in that direction, it cannot regain its former course; what is worse, the longer the relationship lasts, the more persistently both parties simulate their former intimacy and the more strongly they feel that terrible enmity which never develops between strangers but often between people very close to each other. When a relationship has reached such a pass, all one of the parties has to do is tell the other the truth—the whole truth, do you understand? the utter truth—for that truth to turn into an indictment.

If one of the parties tells the whole truth, if he is perfectly honest about how repugnant he finds love's lie, doesn't he thereby force the other party either to admit it tacitly, in which case everything is over and done with, or to fear the consequences so much as to lie doubly, both to himself and to his truthful partner? I am writing now to tell you that truth, and I ask you, beg you, please, darling, don't lie, leave this letter unanswered, honor me with your silence if with nothing else.

First, let me take up your supposed blackout at Yag's. (Is it by chance that blacking out differs from backing out by only one letter?) That was the start of it all, wasn't it? Or to be more accurate, it all started the moment I saw through your blackout and realized you were using it to extricate yourself from a situation that wounded both your self-esteem and my love. Let me note in passing that this explanation fully corroborates my original presentiment that you were ill, an assumption I immediately rejected as worthless (not impossible, simply incorrect).

As you will remember, I took care of you that evening as best I could, bringing you water and wet towels, lavishing tenderness on you, but even then it was all a lie. Even then I thought of you in the third person; in my mind "you" had become "he." Instead of addressing you directly, I had the feeling I was talking about you to someone else, someone suddenly closer to me than you. The "someone" in question was my reason. And that is how I became estranged from you.

But that night I lied; I didn't tell you, couldn't tell you the truth I am writing now: that I was offended. When one person offends another, he does so either intentionally or unintentionally. Intentional offense is nothing terrible: it can be answered with an argument, an insult, a blow, a shot, and, coarse as it may be, it is as easily washed away as dirt in a bath. What is truly awful is offense given unintentionally, unknowingly, with no malice aforethought: if you respond with an insult, an argument, or even simply a look of annoyance, you not only fail to weaken it but offend yourself intolerably. Indeed, what makes unintentional offense so distinctive is that it admits of no response; on the contrary, you must do your utmost to show (and oh, how hard it is) that you haven't noticed a thing. That is why I held my tongue and lied to you that night.

Time after time I asked myself the question and refused to accept the answer. Time after time I asked myself, "What happened?", and time after time I answered, "He didn't want you." Yet even after yielding to the evidence, I failed to understand it. Granted, I would say to myself, he didn't want me. But in that case why did he bother with everything? Why did he arrange for us to meet at Yag's? Why did he act and behave in such a way that his actions and behavior obliged him to take me—and then pull back? Why? There was only one answer: his mind lusted after me, while his body revolted and turned away in disgust. I felt what a leper must feel when a Christian brother kisses him on the lips and vomits immediately thereafter. What I felt in your case, Vadim, was the mind's conscious energy on the one hand and the body's unconscious insubordination on the other. That offended me more than anything else. Be lenient with me, Vadim, and try to understand that any and all rational considerations involved in the physical conquest of a woman are profoundly offensive to her, be they dictated by Christian—and therefore highly spiritual principles—or by base financial ones. Yes. An irrational act performed rationally is an act of ignominy.

You knew my husband was due back the next day. You knew—I told you, after all—that no matter what the consequences I had resolved to give him a full and honest account of everything that had happened in his absence. I did not do so. After that night I did not feel I had the right. What is more, I conceived a new tenderness for him, a new gratitude and intimacy. That is how it was, Vadim, and that is the way you must, the only way you can understand it. For the heart of a female leper beats faster at the sensual kiss of a native than at the Christian kiss of a missionary trying to overcome his disgust.

The day you came to visit, you came as a guest, an outsider. Oh, I know you didn't consider yourself an outsider; you thought you were playing a part and no one could be closer to me than you. But I also know how wrong you were, and believe it or not, Vadimushka, I suddenly felt sorry for you and your self-assurance, painfully sorry. It all began when my husband, who had clearly taken a liking to you, asked for my arm and, with his usual lack of tact, took you on a tour of the flat.

I must tell you that my husband is not the jealous type, a phenomenon that may be explained by an excess of self-assurance and a dearth of imagination. Yet these very qualities would have provoked him to extreme cruelty had he learned of my betrayal. My husband has no doubt whatever that he and he alone is the point around which all humanity revolves. He is absolutely incapable of seeing that every other human being feels the same way and that from the standpoint of each of those "every others," he, my husband, not only was deprived of his pointhood but was himself forced to revolve; in other words, my husband cannot comprehend that the world of many such central points, each supporting its own self-perceived, self-defined subworld, is equal to the number of living creatures in that world. Though recognizing the human *I* as the center or navel of the world, my husband has succeeded in locating it only within himself. Everyone else for him is *you, he,* or, more generally, *they*. Thus, while calling his *I* supremely human, he fails to understand that it is in fact purely animal and would be more at home in a boa constrictor swallowing a rabbit or, for that matter, the rabbit it swallows. My husband does not realize that a basic difference between animal mentality and human mentality lies in the fact that when an animal admits the existence of an external *I* it admits physical inferiority and therefore defeat, whereas when a human admits the existence of an external *I* he celebrates spiritual superiority and therefore a great victory.

Now that you know what my husband is like, you understand what a pity it is that circumstances have forced me to stay with him. A blow to his thick skull in the form of living proof I had betrayed him, preferred someone else to him, would have done him a world of good.

But to return to your visit. You remember, of course, the inevitable moment when we reached the door of our bedroom. You remember my reticence, my refusal to open the door and my husband's blind rage when, after throwing open the door himself and pushing me inside, he called back to you, "Come in, come in. This is our bedroom. All mahogany." You peered in, saw the unmade bed, the bedclothes in wild disarray at nine o'clock in the evening, and you understood. I know the jealousy, the pain you must have felt standing there seeing your love ridiculed and defiled; I knew it then. Not until later did I learn that the birth of your sensuality coincided with the defilement of your love. What a shame I learned it too late.

Even though I continued seeing you behind my husband's back, our rendezvous were different. Each time we met you would take me to a filthy slum, tear off my clothes and yours, and take me more coarsely, ruthlessly, cynically. Don't blame me for letting you have your way. Don't try to tell me you gave me a moment of pleasure. I endured depravity the way a patient endures medicine: he dreams of saving his life; I dreamt of saving my love. At first—even though I noticed, even though I realized that your sensuality grew more inflamed the more your love cooled—I hoped and waited for something. But yesterday, yesterday I felt, I understood that even the sensuality had gone out of you, that you had had your fill, that I was superfluous, that there was no point in keeping up pretenses.

When you took me up to that hole in the wall above the restaurant yesterday, you didn't bother to kiss me or put your arms around me, you didn't say a word of greeting; you simply started taking off your clothes with the equanimity of a civil servant arriving at work in the morning. I watched you standing there before me in—excuse me—not the cleanest of underwear, meticulously folding your trousers; watched you walk over to the washstand, remove the towel, tuck it away prudently under the pillow. Later, when it was all over, you took it out, nonchalantly cleaned yourself off with it, and, after suggesting I do the same, turned your back and lit a cigarette.

"Is that the love I was ready to leave everything for, to ruin my life for?" I asked myself. No, Vadim, no, my dearest, it wasn't love at all; it was a foul, a loathsome mire. I have enough of that mire at home not to bring more back to my all-mahogany conjugal bed from the fusty back room of some dive or other. And cruel as it may seem to you, Vadim, I must say that if I have come to prefer my husband to you it is not only for what he offers but for what he is. Yes, Vadim, all things considered, I prefer my husband to you. Look at it as I do. My husband's erotic nature is the result of a constitutional poverty of the spirit and, as such, has no power to offend. Your relationship to me is a kind of unending fall, a constant impoverishment of the emotions, which, like all forms of impoverishment, humiliates more the more the riches it supplants.

Farewell, Vadim. Farewell, my dearest, my darling little boy. Farewell, my dream, my chimera, my fool's paradise. Believe me: you are young, you have your whole life ahead of you, *you* will still be happy. Farewell.

Sonya

COCAINE

1

It was no longer possible to stretch out on the windowsill, a dark-gray slab of stone artificially veined to look like marble but with a white edge planed down from sharpening penknives, no longer possible to stretch out on it and crane one's neck to see the long, narrow asphalt path that ran through the fence-enclosed courtyard. The fence, though always locked, could be entered by means of a wicket hanging from a rusty hinge as if heavy with fatigue. The tenants were forever tripping on its lower bar and casting injurious glances back at it.

It was winter. The windows were caulked with a cream-colored putty, and between the uprights of the window frames lay a rounded mass of cotton wool and two tall, narrow beakers of a yellow liquid. Walking up to the window from force of summer habit and feeling the dry heat steam up from below the sill, I felt more cut off than ever from the street, which radiated either well-being or depression depending on my mood. The only things I could see now from my tiny room were the neighboring wall, where gray trickles of whitewash had frozen on the bricks, and the fenced-in area below, which our doorkeeper, Matvei, pompously called the "Masters' Garden," though all one had to do was glance at garden or masters to see that the great respect Matvei lavished upon them was nothing more than a calculated ruse to enhance his own dignity at the expense of his superiors'.

For the previous few months I had had particularly frequent bouts of depression. I would stand at the window for long periods of time, a cigarette in the catapult of my fingers, and try to count—through the deep-blue smoke from the tangerine tip and the filthy gray smoke from the cardboard filter—the number of bricks in the neighboring wall; or, at night, having switched off the lamp and the dark reflection of the room in the suddenly brighter windowpane, I would watch, head back, the thickly falling flurries until I seemed to be rising along a lift of immobile cords of snow; or else, after wandering aimlessly up and down the passageway, I would open the door, walk out into the cold stairway, and—wondering whom I might ring up, though knowing full well I had no reason to ring anyone at all—go downstairs to the telephone.

There at the main entrance, his boots propped up on the rung of the stool, sat our carrot-top Matvei wearing a dark-blue coat gathered at the back in an accordion pleat and a cap with a gold band. Stroking his knees with his enormous hands, as if having just given them a wallop, he would throw his head back and yawn—that is, open his mouth in a terrible gape to reveal a raised and fluttering tongue—and emit an anguished roar that mounted *oo-aa-ee* up the scale and descended *ee-aa-oo* back down. Once the yawn was over, but before the tears of sleep had disappeared, he would give his head a self-reproachful shake and rub his face with his enormous hands as though giving it a brisk, invigorating wash. The most likely explanation for Matvei's tendency to yawn was that the tenants avoided his services whenever possible. Many years ago they had installed a system of bells running from the telephone booth to each and every flat, so that all Matvei had to do when anyone received a call was to press the proper button.

The signal summoning me down to the telephone was a single long, agonizing peal, but it had taken on overtones of joy and excitement when, as of late, the summonses came more and more rarely.

Yag was in love and spent all his time with his flame, an older woman with a Spanish look about her. For some reason she had taken an instant dislike to me, and he and I rarely saw each other anymore.

I had tried several times to renew my acquaintance with Burkewitz, but stopped seeing him altogether when it proved impossible for the two of us to find a common language. Burkewitz had become a revolutionary, and the only way to talk to him was to wax indignant over the civic sins of others or confess one's own sins against the commonweal. I found his attitude odious and humiliating. While I was accustomed to hiding my feelings behind a veil of cynicism or, at best, making a joke of them, Burkewitz used his highflown ideals to condemn both humor and cynicism: humor, because he felt the presence of cynicism in it, and cynicism, because he felt the absence of humor in it.

The only one left was Stein, who did, in fact, phone from time to time and ask me over. I invariably accepted his invitations.

Stein lived in a luxurious house with marble staircases and raspberry-colored runners, with an elegantly attentive doorkeeper and a lift that smelled of perfume and raced up so fast that the always unexpected and unpleasant jolt accompanying each stop made one's heart continue upwards for a moment before falling back to its proper place. No sooner did the housemaid open the enormous white lacquered door, no sooner was I enveloped by the soft sounds and fragrances of the large and extremely expensive flat, than Stein would come running out to greet me as if in a terrible rush and, taking me by the arm, drag me quickly into his room.

Having offered me a seat but never taking one himself, Stein would immediately start going through in his wardrobe, fumbling in the pockets of his suits, and sometimes even running out into the entrance hall and rummaging about in his fur coats and overcoats. Not until he was satisfied he had missed nothing would he place the objects of his search on the desk before me. They were all old ticket stubs, printed invitations, handbills for plays, concerts, and balls, in other words, tangible evidence of where he had been—at which premieres, in which theaters, in which row—and, most important, how much being there had cost him. After laying them all out in such a manner as to ensure they made a progressively greater impression on me—ticket price being his sole criterion—he would begin, screwing his eyes up languidly as if to gather the strength to perform a terribly tedious duty with honor, to tell his tale.

Never saying a word about how the actors had performed or whether the play had been worthwhile, the orchestra or soloists up to standard, never giving any indication of the feelings he had come away with, Stein would go into the minutest of details about what the audience was like, which of his acquaintances he had seen, which row they were sitting in, who was sitting with Stockholder A's mistress in his box, where and with whom Banker B was sitting, the names of the people he, Stein, had been introduced to on that particular evening, and how much his new acquaintances amassed (Stein never used the word "earn") in a year. Doubtless, he, like our doorkeeper Matvei, sincerely believed his image enhanced in my eyes by the incomes and high posts of his acquaintances. Once he had gone through his comments with a kind of torpid vanity, repeating how hard it was to find tickets and how much extra he had had to pay the middleman, he would lean over me and underline an astronomical box-office price with the finely manicured nail of his flat, white thumb. Then, pausing for a moment and inviting me thereby to raise my eyes from the ticket to himself, he would spread his arms, tilt his head to one shoulder, and smile a pitiful smile as if to say he was so amused by the inordinate price of the ticket that he couldn't bring himself to be outraged by it.

Sometimes I would arrive to find him shaving, ducking in and out of the bathroom, scurrying about on his long, spindly legs in a feverish rush. Since on such occasions he was invariably on his way to a ball or a party or a visit or a concert, I found it odd that he should have felt the need to summon me urgently by phone.

Scattering things all over the place, whether he needed them for the evening or not, he would hastily hold them up for me to see—socks, handkerchiefs, braces, cravats, cologne—dropping price and place of purchase as he went.

Fully dressed in silk-lined fur coat and pointed beaver hat, he would preen before the mirror, knitting his red brows from the fumes of a newly lit cigar, running a hand over his freshly shaven and powdered neck, and (as always while looking in the mirror) turning down the corners of his mouth like a fish. Then, with a curt "All right, let's go," he would tear his eyes from his image, march briskly to the door, and race down the softly sighing runners at such a pace that I could scarcely keep up with him. I don't know why, but there was something terribly offensive and shameful, something humiliating in the way I ran after him. Downstairs in front of the main entrance, where a first-class carriage stood waiting, he would say a cold good-bye, proffering a flaccid hand and withdrawing it immediately, then turn, climb into the cab, and drive off.

I remember once asking him to lend me some money—a pittance, several rubles. Screwing up his eyes as if to protect them from smoke, though he was not smoking at the time, and saying not a word, he extracted a wallet of striated silk from his side pocket with a grandiloquent gesture and pulled out a crisp new hundred-ruble note. "Is he really going to give it to me?" I wondered. And oddly enough, much as I needed the money, I felt sorely disillusioned: for wasn't a good deed done by a scoundrel as disappointing as a base deed done by a man of high ideals?

But Stein did not give me the money. "It's all I've got," he said, pointing his chin at it. "If it were in smaller denominations, I'd of course let you have as much as ten rubles. But as it is, I can't see my way to changing it, not even if all you need is ten kopecks." And while he spoke, his cold, faded eyes, concentrating as usual on my face instead of my eyes, sought in vain what they had expected to see. "A hundred rubles in change is not the same as a hundred-ruble note," he went on, clearly running out of patience, yet pausing for some reason to hold up the other side of his hand. "Once a banknote has been broken into, it has lost its innocence and is as good as lost."

"Of course, of course," I said, nodding gleefully and smiling, trying as best I could to hide my humiliation, for I knew that by letting it be seen (oh, how right Sonya was, how right she was) I would only have exacerbated it.

Stein opened his arms wide and struck an attitude combining reproach (he had been doubted) and satisfaction (he had been vindicated). "Gentlemen," he said complacently, "the time has come. The time has come at last for you to act like Europeans, for you to understand these things."

Even though I was quite a frequent visitor, Stein never took the trouble to introduce me to his parents. True, if Stein had come to see me, I would not have introduced him to my mother, but similar attitudes can hide diametrically opposed motives. Stein did not introduce me to his parents because he was ashamed of me; I did not introduce Stein to my mother because I was ashamed of her. And every time I came home from Stein's, I was tormented by the humiliation of the poor, whose feeling of spiritual superiority is too strong to envy the rich openly, yet too weak to ignore them.

It is curious how the most antagonistic of forces attract one another with an all but irresistible power. A man is, say, having dinner, when suddenly, somewhere behind his back, a dog begins to vomit. The man may continue his meal and pay no attention. He may stop eating and walk away without looking. He may. But he feels a nagging force, a temptation of sorts (though what sort of temptation could it be?), prompting him to turn his head and steal a glance, even though he has no desire whatever to see what the glance will reveal, even though he knows it will send shivers of repulsion up his spine.

Such was the nagging force I felt in connection with Stein. Each time I came home from his place, I would swear never to set foot there again. But hearing his voice over the phone a few days later, I would go to see him—go to feed my repulsion, as it were. Many was the time when, lying in my room with the lights out, I imagined myself running a business, an extremely successful business, even opening my own bank, while Stein—in tatters, impoverished, and bursting with envy—made up to me. I found those dreams and visions extraordinarily pleasant, though (contradictory as it may seem) the pleasure I derived from them was singularly unpleasant.

Be that as it may, I leapt joyfully from my couch one evening at the sound of the long, raging bell summoning me to the phone. On that fateful, terrible evening I was willing once more to go and do Stein's bidding, but I was in for a surprise. When, having raced down the cold staircase and into the sweat-and-powder-scented booth, I picked up the receiver, which hung almost to the ground by a long, green, twisted cord, the hoarse whisper that emerged belonged not to Stein but to Zander, a student I had recently met in an office at the university. And this Zander began barking something in my ear about a sniffing session he and a friend had set up for that evening. "A what?" I asked him, not understanding, and he explained it meant they would be taking cocaine. They were low on funds and wondered whether I couldn't help them out. They'd wait for me at the café.

I had only the vaguest idea of what cocaine was like. For some reason I associated it with alcohol (at least in terms of the danger it posed to the organism). And since on that evening, as on every other for that matter, I had no idea what to do with myself or where to go, and since I happened to have fifteen rubles, I accepted the invitation with glee.

2

The frost was hard and dry. Everything felt ready to crack. As the sleigh pulled up to the arcade, I heard high-pitched metallic steps on all sides and saw smoke rising in white columns from all the roofs. The city seemed to hang in the sky like a gigantic icon-lamp.

The arcade, too, was very cold and resonant, and all the mirrors were coated with snow, but no sooner did I open the door to the café than a washhouse cloud of warmth, odor, and sound wafted over me. The tiny cloakroom, which was separated from the café proper by no more than a partition, was so crammed with coats one on top of the other that the doorkeeper huffed and puffed as if on his way up a mountain when, grabbing the waist of the coat he had just removed from me, he blindly dragged it along the pegs, unable to keep the collar from falling back on him, much less find space to hang it. There were columns of hats and caps piled along the upper shelf and in front of the mirror, and boots and galoshes below, stuffed one into the other, with identification numbers scribbled on the soles in chalk.

Just as I squeezed my way into the main room, the violinist, his instrument under his chin, lifted the bow with a flourish, rose up on his toes and hunched his shoulders forward, and, coming down suddenly (and pulling the piano and cello along with him), began to play.

Still standing near the musicians, I looked out into the teeming room, where the general voice level had markedly increased the moment the musicians struck up, and tried to locate Zander. The pianist at my side gave his elbows, shoulder blades, and entire back such a good workout that the chair, the dog-eared old score that was serving to keep the chair legs even, and the chair's loose back were all in constant motion; the cellist, his face mellowed by a pair of raised eyebrows, kept an ear cocked in the direction of whatever finger happened to be rocking back and forth on the string; and the violinist, legs spread wide and torso writhing with impatient passion, radiated an embarrassingly lascivious pleasure in his own sonorities, though his joyfully insistent attempts to attract attention went absolutely ignored.

Rising up on my toes and pulling in my stomach, I weaved my way through the jammed together tables, and as I went I found myself trying—and failing, of course (I seemed to have developed a need to prove my intellectual incompetence to myself)—to come up with a definition of music. Here on the other side of the café, where there was a bit more space, sounds changed direction like the wind, sometimes altogether abandoning the musicians, whose bows then sawed in silence. It was here, near an enormous window, towering high over the heads of the customers and waving a handkerchief to catch my eye, that Zander finally came into sight.

"There you are at last!" he cried, elbowing his way up to greet me. "There you are at last!" And grabbing my hand in both of his, he added, "How've you been, Vadya?" Then his head shook slightly, and he said again, "How've you been?" Zander's head had a habit of shaking, after which everything he had said would shake loose, fly away, and with tedious obstinacy he would say it again.

Screwing up his sharp eyes and rapacious nose and never letting go of my hand, he dragged me to a table occupied by two others. From the expectant way they looked me in the eye I could tell that they were part of Zander's party and that he was about to introduce us. After both of them had stood, Zander presented one as Hirghe and the other as Mik, and since his head shook three times, he had to explain three times that Mik was a cartoonist and dancer. About Hirghe he said nothing, but Hirghe could be easily characterized in two words: indolent disgust. When we came up to the table, he stood with indolent disgust, he gave me his hand with indolent disgust, and, taking his seat, he looked out over the heads of the crowd with indolent disgust. Mik, the other one, was clearly the nervous type. A cigarette dangling from his lips, he turned to Zander without so much as looking at me and said, "Let's get down to business, shall we? How do things stand? Tell us how things stand." And learning from Zander that as things stood they had fifteen rubles at their disposal, he first made a sour face, then gave a smile, and finally erased all emotion from his features and started tapping his ring loudly against the glass tabletop.

In response to the tapping noise a waitress with a frightfully emaciated face that immediately struck me as familiar turned and, pushing her starched apron into the sharp table corner, began clearing the empty glasses. Not until she got round to clearing the cigarette butts—which, for want of an ashtray, were strewn across the table and made her turn down the corners of her mouth squeamishly and shake her head as if to say she expected nothing better from the likes of us—not until then did I realize who she was: Nelly.

When I greeted her and asked how she'd been getting along, her cheeks broke out in brick-red splotches and she murmured "*Bien, merci,*" without so much as a glance in my direction, still wiping off the table with her rag. After she had cleared it entirely, she stole a frightened look in the direction of the counter, leaned over to Hirghe, and whispered that her shift was almost up and that she would wait for them downstairs. Whereupon Hirghe, pressing his hands against the table with a face so distorted from the effort that one would think he had just sustained a severe back injury, gave a nod of indolent disgust.

3

Before a quarter hour had elapsed, all of us—Nelly, Zander, Mik, and I—had settled down to wait for Hirghe in his well-heated room. (Hirghe himself was off somewhere fetching the cocaine: I'd been informed on the way that Hirghe was a pusher, not a snorter.) The room was decorated with extremely old furniture. Immediately behind the door—and so close to it that the door would open only halfway—stood a rickety upright with keys the color of unbrushed teeth. A pair of drooping candlesticks screwed directly into the piano's bosom sported a pair of red, golden-flecked, white-wicked, spiral candles which, since the openings in the candlesticks were too large, pointed off in different directions. Next along the wall came a fireplace with a white marble mantelpiece, a bell jar on the mantelpiece, and two bronze Frenchmen under the bell jar. The gentlemen, arrayed in doublets, hose, and buckled pumps, were leaning forward, executing a *pas de menuet* while preparing to toss a clock elegantly into the air; the clock had a white dial but no glass, a black hole for winding but no key, and only one hand, which was badly bent out of shape. In the middle of the room were some low armchairs upholstered in a velvet which when rubbed with the nap appeared yellow and when rubbed against it appeared black—so distinctly black, in fact, that one could write on it; and in the middle of the armchairs under a droplight was an oval table, finished in black lacquer, its ornately curved legs united by a strip of wood with a family album lying on it, or at least so I realized the moment I pulled it out.

The album was sealed by a clasp, but when I pushed the button on the clasp it opened with a jolt. The binding was made of purple velvet fastened in each lower corner by rounded copper nails that made the album seem to be resting on tiny rollers, while the upper part of the binding was decorated with a representation, in peeling paint, of a driver cracking his whip over a troika as it flew through the clouds. I had just opened the album and was starting to look through the gilt-edged pages, which were so thick that they clacked like wood as I turned them, when Mik called out to me from the far end of the room, "Take a gander at this, why don't you!"

He was standing looking the other way and summoning me with a hand stretched out behind him. "Feast your eyes on the little bastard! What a fright!" He pointed to a naked bronze cherub balancing an enormous candlestick in his chubby little hand. "It pains me to think of how benighted the people who made him must have been," he said, pressing a clenched fist to his forehead, "to say nothing of the people who bought him. Have a look at him, my boy, have a good look"—and here he grabbed me by the shoulder—"at his face. Just think,"—and here he pressed his fist to his forehead again—"this little sapling is holding in his outstretched hand an object five times heavier than his own weight. Why, it's monstrous! That would be like you or me holding up a thousand pounds! And what does his little face tell us? Do you see the slightest trace of effort or strain? All you'd have to do is saw the candlestick off his hand and, believe me, you wouldn't be able to tell by looking at his face whether he was about to go to sleep or to . . . Horrors, horrors!"

"What's wrong now?" Zander cried out gleefully from the other end of the room. He had just started making his way round the armchairs in our direction when in came Hirghe. He was wearing a smock and clutching something carefully to his breast, and the moment he entered the room—no, the moment he kicked the door open with his knee—Mik, Zander, and Nelly all ran up to him. Since he showed no sign of stopping, they trooped behind him to the black lacquered table, where they could see better under the droplight. I joined them.

Already waiting on the table was a small tin box much like the ones toffee comes in at Abrikosov's only smaller, its shiny, almost polished-looking surface spotted with scraps of glued-on paper. Next to the box lay something that resembled a pair of dividers and next to that—another small box, made of wood.

"Well, let's get going, let's get going. What are we waiting for?" said Mik. "Look at our beauty here. She can hardly stand it." He nodded at the suddenly haggard Nelly, who—now leaning her elbows on the table, now sitting up straight—never took her eyes off Hirghe, as if trying to judge where best to sink her teeth into him.

As for Hirghe, he merely wiped his forehead wearily and, scarcely moving his tongue or lips, said with repugnance, "The price of a gram today is seven rubles fifty. How much do you want?" These last words were addressed to me, and seeing Zander give me an indignant wink that seemed to say "I went to all that trouble to teach you your role, and now you've forgotten it," I replied that I had just under fifteen rubles.

"And I get a gram," Nelly interjected unexpectedly and bit down on her lower lip with such intensity that it turned white.

Hirghe lowered his eyes and bent his head forward ever so slightly in agreement. Then he put his lit cigarette down on the edge of the table and, paying no heed whatever to Mik—who had let out a deep breath and was showing his impatience by pacing the room, head in hands—opened the tin box. "So you want two grams, right?" he said to me while starting to extract a blue object from it.

"What do you mean?!" Zander cried out, stopping him. "We're in this together!" Then his head shook, and he repeated, "We're in this together!"

At this point Mik ran up to the table, his index finger raised as if he had just had a brilliant idea, and with a voice full of glee proposed that the three grams be divided into four parts, in other words, that each of us receive three fourths of a gram.

"No, I get a whole gram," said Nelly petulantly, her eyes on the ground. "I slave a whole day, I get a whole gram." She bit hard into her lip again.

"All right, all right," said Mik in a tone combining reconciliation with irritation, "we'll do it differently." And he suggested dividing up my two grams by giving Zander and himself each three quarters of a gram and me, a neophyte, half a gram. "You don't mind, do you?" he asked, looking me tenderly in the eye. All that remained was to prove to Zander that two three-quarters plus one half did indeed add up to two.

Seeing that unanimity had at last been reached, Hirghe perked up and took the money from Nelly and me, counted it carefully, and slipped it into his pocket. Then, moving his cigarette so as not burn the table, he picked up the box with the blue object in it. As he lifted it out of the box, I realized that it was a tiny cone of dark blue paper and that the instrument next to the now empty box, the instrument I had taken for a pair of dividers, was in fact a set of apothecary scales. From his waistcoat pocket Hirghe took a tiny ivory scoop and some small squares of paper folded as pharmacists fold paper for powders. He opened one of the squares—it was empty—and placed it in one of the scalepans, and putting a minuscule weight (the other box contained the weights) on the other one, he raised the beam of the scales high enough for the wires to grow taut but not so high that the pans left the table. Still holding the scales in one hand, he used the other hand, the one that held the ivory scoop, to open the blue cone and plunge the scoop into it. I heard a rustling of paper and noticed another cone tucked into the blue one, a whitish cone made of something like waxed paper (which was what had made the rustling noise). When the scoop emerged slowly from the cone, it had a small mound of white powder on it. It was very white and had a crystalline gleam to it, much like naphthalene. Hirghe very carefully flicked the powder on the square of paper with one hand and raised the beam with the other. The pan with the weight proved heavier. Then, without releasing the scales, he inserted the ivory scoop back into the cone, but apparently had trouble manipulating it.

"Come and hold the cone," he said to Mik, who happened to be standing closest. It was only after hearing him speak that I realized how terribly quiet the room had become.

"Why, there's almost nothing left!" cried Mik, while Hirghe, ignoring him completely, loaded the scoop with cocaine and flicked it from scoop to scale as if flicking the ashes off a cigarette.

As soon as the beam balanced, Hirghe returned the rest of the cocaine from the scoop with a single meticulous flick, put down the scales, and picked up the square of paper with the power in it. Then he packed it down a bit, thereby increasing its sheen, and, after folding it together, held it out to Nelly.

While Hirghe was at work preparing the next packet—he usually sold them pre-packed, but Mik, fearing, as I later learned, that Hirghe would adulterate it with quinine, had made it a condition of purchase that he be present at the time the cocaine was measured out—in any case, while Hirge was at work preparing the next packet, I kept my eye on Nelly. She immediately opened her own packet, took a short, narrow glass tube out of her handbag, and used the tip to push aside a tiny mound of cocaine, which crumbled on the spot. Next she placed one end of the tube just above the mound, bent her head forward, inserted the other end of the tube into her right nostril, and inhaled. Even though the glass never made contact with the cocaine, the mound disappeared. Having repeated the process with the left nostril, she folded the square of paper, put it away carefully in her handbag, and went off to the back of the room to make herself comfortable in one of the armchairs.

In the meantime, Hirghe had weighed out the next packet, and Zander had begun hovering over him. "Oh, don't bother to fold it," he said while Hirghe, cocking his head to one side as if admiring his handiwork, put the finishing touches on it. "You needn't make a neat little pile or tamp it down," he added, his quivering hand grabbing the open square of paper from Hirghe's calm one. Zander quickly poured a small mound of cocaine—but quite a bit larger than Nelly's—on the back of his hand. Next, stretching his hairy neck in such a way that it remained above the table, Zander brought his nose down to the cocaine and, without touching it, twisted his mouth to close one nostril, and inhaled noisily. The mound disappeared from his hand. He did the same thing with the other nostril, the only difference being that the amount of cocaine he set aside for it was so insignificant I could scarcely see it. "I can only take it with my left nostril," he explained with a look of perplexity, in the manner of a man who, while telling you how special he is, tries to temper his claims. Then, wrinkling his forehead in disgust and sticking out his tongue as far as it would go, he licked the spot on his hand where the cocaine had been, and even bent over and licked a spot on the table when he spied a speck of powder that had fallen from his nose. The dull, wet circle made by his tongue on the lacquered finish quickly disappeared.

By then my dose had been weighed out and lay in a neat packet before me, but I kept my eyes on Mik, who, having closed the door after the departing Hirghe, was pouring his powder with great care into a tiny glass phial he had taken from his pocket. After sniffing (he, too, had his own way of going about it: inserting the flat end of a toothpick into the phial and prying loose the cocaine that had stuck needle-like to the wall, he withdrew the toothpick with a miniature pyramid balanced on it, and raised it to his nose without spilling a grain), he noticed my untouched supply.

"And what are *you* waiting for?" he asked me with a combination of reproach and puzzlement, as if I were reading a newspaper in the foyer of a theater after the play had begun.

I told him I didn't know how and hadn't the proper equipment.

"Come over here. I'll take care of everything," he said, as if I had no ticket and he were willing to give me one. "Nelly! Zander!" he called out to his companions, who, having found some chalk and a pack of cards, were setting up a card table in a corner of the room. "Stop what you're doing. Come and watch. I mean, how often do you see a man lose his nasal virginity?"

He opened the packet (the cocaine had been flattened somewhat inside—thicker in the center, it thinned along the sides to a wavy line—and when Mik opened the packet, it split down the middle with a start), gathered up a bit of the powder on the end of his toothpick, and putting his arm around my shoulders, drew me slightly closer to him. Now I could see his face up close. His eyes were moist but flaming, sparkling; his lips, though closed, were in constant motion, as if sucking on a fruit drop. "All you have to do is breathe in when I bring this little snort up to your nostril," he said, carefully lifting the toothpick.

But when, feeling it approach, I went to take a breath, Mik suddenly let out a "Damn!" and dropped his arm: the toothpick was empty.

"Look what you've done!" Zander exclaimed (he

and Nelly had come up to the table in the meantime). "You've blown it off."

I found it strange that even while holding my breath I could have blown the cocaine quite away. But then I noticed that just below my chin my jacket was covered with the white powder. I started brushing it off mechanically, with my sleeve, as one brushes off a bit of fluff.

"What are you doing now, you idiot?" Zander cried, dropping to his knees with a thud and immediately gathering the grains into his own packet.

Sensing that I had committed a terrible faux pas, I threw a beseeching glance at Nelly.

"Don't worry, don't worry," she responded soothingly. "You just haven't got the hang of it." She leaned over the table and took the toothpick from Mik's hands, then (circumventing Zander—who was still crawling about the floor—with a sibilant, peasant-like "Saints preserve us!") came up to me. "You see, darling, you see, my sweet," she said, waving the toothpick (she was having a little trouble enunciating, as if something were keeping her from opening her mouth), "cocaine or 'coke,' as it's called for short, just plain coke, you see? Well, anyway, coke . . ."

"Or cocaine, as it's called for long," Mik broke in, but Nelly waved him off with the toothpick.

"So anyway, coke," she went on, "is incredibly, I mean, devilishly light. You know what I mean? The slightest puff and it vanishes into thin air. That's why you've got to breathe out, what I mean is, exhale beforehand."

"From the lungs, naturally," a morose Mik interjected.

"From the lungs," cooed Nelly. Then, turning to Mik: "Oh, clear off, will you? You're just in the way."

And back to me: "So now you understand. As soon the stuff gets up near your nose, no more breathi One quick sniff. Now you understand, right?" As s spoke, she loaded a mound of cocaine on the too pick.

Obeying her commands, I held my breath a then inhaled as soon as I felt the tickle of the toothpi near my nostril.

"Perfect," said Nelly. "Now once more." And on more she dug the toothpick into the powder.

I felt nothing in my nose from the first sniff, e cept perhaps—when I gave my nose a slight pull— momentary smell of the apothecary, an unusual but n unpleasant smell that dissipated the instant I breathe it in. When I sensed the toothpick coming up to m other nostril, I again ingested it through my nose, bu this time, more confident, I breathed in much mor powerfully. Apparently, however, I went too far: as soon as the powder passed the nasal passages, I automatically swallowed it and immediately felt a sharp, vile, bitter taste rise up from my throat and mix with the saliva in my mouth.

Conscious of Nelly's probing eyes, I tried not to make a face. The eyes, usually dirty blue, were now quite black, with only the thinnest of blue lines encircling their wildly dilated, fiery pupils. Meanwhile, her lips, lik Mik's, kept up a constant sucking motion; and I was jus about to ask what they were sucking on when Nelly, wh had given Mik his toothpick back and put my packet i order, moved off quickly in the direction of the doo turned and said, "I'll only be a minute," and went ou

The bitter taste in my mouth was almost gon and all that remained was an ice-cold feeling in m throat and gums, the kind of feeling that comes whe during a frost, one closes one's mouth after breathi

with it open and the warm saliva makes it even colder. My teeth were completely frozen, and if I put pressure on any one of them, I felt the others follow painlessly, as if they were all soldered together.

"Breathe only through your nose now," Mik told me, and, indeed, I found it so easy to breathe that the openings in my nose seemed to have grown extraordinarily large and the air smelled unusually rich and fresh. "No, no, no," he said, reaching out, frightened, to stop me when he saw the handkerchief I had taken out of my pocket. "Put it away. It's against the rules," he said in no uncertain terms.

"But what if I have to blow my nose?" I insisted.

"What a thing to say!" he replied, sticking out his neck and pressing his fist to his forehead. "You'd have to be an imbecile to blow your nose after a snort! Who has ever heard of such a thing. Swallow. That's cocaine you've taken, not a cold remedy."

Meanwhile, Zander, who had been sitting on the edge of a chair, packet in hand, gave his head a sudden shake and went up to the door as though he had just come to a decision. "Do me a favor, Zander," said Mik just before he went out. "Knock on the door and tell Nelly to get a move on. And don't take your time either. I'm not dead yet, you know."

When Zander, with exaggerated, even fearful caution, had closed the door behind him, I asked Mik what was wrong and where they were all going.

"Oh, it's nothing, really," he answered. (He, too, was now talking strangely, through his teeth.) "The first snorts upset your stomach a little. But it doesn't last long and doesn't come back before the end of the session." He listened at the door for a moment and added, comfortingly, "You have a while yet."

"I don't think the cocaine is going to have any

effect on me at all," I blurted out, but the pure ring of my voice gave me such pleasure that I was under the impression I had said something terribly clever.

Making a special trip across the room to give me a condescending pat on the shoulder, Mik said to me, "Do tell, do tell." And with a nasty smile on his face he went back to the door, opened it, and stepped out.

4

Now I am alone in the room. I go and sit by the fireplace. I sit by the black, grate-covered maw of the fireplace and do what anyone in my place and position would do: I strain my consciousness to observe the changes taking place in my sensations. It is an indispensable means of self-defense, a dam I set up between my inner feelings and their outward manifestation.

Mik, Nelly, and Zander come back into the room. I undo my packet on the arm of the chair, ask Mik for his toothpick, and take two more snorts. Not for me, of course; for them. The paper crackles, the cocaine jumps, but I get through it all without spilling a speck. I attribute the slight rush of joy I feel in the process to my new dexterity.

I sprawl out in the chair. I feel good. An exploratory ray inside me illuminates my sensations. I wait for them to explode, to send out drug-induced flashes of lightning, but the longer I wait the more I am convinced that no explosion or flash is forthcoming or ever will be. In other words, I am immune to cocaine. And the idea that so potent a poison is impotent when faced with the likes of me augments and reinforces my joy by making me feel exceptional.

Zander and Nelly are sitting at the card table on the other side of the room tossing cards back and forth. Mik slaps one pocket after another until he finds some matches, and lights one of the candles. I look on lovingly as he cups it in his hand, focusing the light on his face.

And all the while I feel better and better. I feel new joy welling up within me, feel it tucking its tender head into my throat and tickling it. Before long (I am having a little trouble breathing) I can't contain myself for joy, I feel it running over, I have a burning desire to tell these poor little people a story.

It makes no difference that they keep shushing me, waving at me, telling me to keep quiet (we have agreed to observe the strictest silence). I don't take it amiss. For an instant, but only the shortest of instants, I perceive a potential insult. But the anticipation of an insult and the surprise when it does not come—these no longer rank as experience; they are, rather, theoretical conclusions about feelings which, given the events, I ought to have. The joy within me has grown so strong it can pass unscathed through any humiliation. It is like a cloud: it cannot be scratched by the sharpest knife.

Mik plays a chord. My body twitches. Only now do I realize how stiff it is. I am sitting *up* in my chair, not *back* in it, and my stomach muscles are unpleasantly taut. I try leaning back, but it doesn't help. Here I sit in a soft, comfortable chair and I am so terribly tense that I can't help feeling it is about to fall apart under me.

The candle above Mik's head is burning brightly, the flickering tongue of its flame casting a mustache-like shadow under his nose. He plays another chord, then repeats it immediately but more softly. I can feel him floating away with the room.

"*Now* see if you can come up with a definition of music," my lips whisper, and the joy in my throat rolls up into a hysterical, bouncing little ball. "Music is the simultaneous representation in sound of the emotion of motion and the motion of emotion." Over and over I whisper these words with my lips, imbuing them with more and more, deeper and deeper meaning, until I am spent with ecstasy.

I make a great effort to sigh, but I am still so tense, so keyed-up that although I take a deep breath I let it out in short puffs. I want to lift the packet from the arm of the chair and take some more, but even after concentrating all my strength of will on ordering my hands to move quickly, I cannot make them obey, and they move slowly, reluctantly, petrified by a fear of breaking, spilling, or capsizing something.

Having sat thus—listing slightly, one leg over the other—for quite some time, I feel a need to relieve the heavy, numb fatigue that has invaded me. Again I strain my will, try to move, turn, sit a different way, lean my weight on the other hip, but my body is petrified, frozen, chained: one move and everything will come tumbling down with a bang. I feel more and more frustrated by my inability to overcome, destroy this frightening paralysis, yet the frustration itself is mute, buried, impossible to vent, and thus constantly growing.

"Our friend Vadim looks pretty far gone." That is Mik talking.

Then comes an interval during which I can tell they are all looking at me. I sit paralyzed, without turning my head. I still have the feeling that by doing so I will turn the room upside down.

"Not in the least. It's just a reaction. All he needs is a quick snort." That is Nelly speaking.

Mik comes over to me. I hear him opening the packet just above my ear, but do not look up. I look away, look down, do everything I can to prevent him from seeing my eyes. I am afraid to show them to anyone. It is a new sensation. It has nothing to do with shyness or timidity; no, it is a fear of humiliation, of shame, and of something else, something absolutely terrifying that is there for all to see. I feel the toothpick near my nostril and inhale. Then once more.

I want to communicate my gratitude, but my voice will not come. Before I can get out a "Thank you," I have to go through a fit of coughing, and the voice that emerges is not my own; it is dull and laborious, strained through clenched teeth.

Mik is still at my side. "Is there anything else you need?" he asks. I nod. I am moving more easily; I am much looser. The dull irritation has been replaced by a fresh surge of joy.

Mik takes me by the arm. I stand. I walk. At first, it is a bit difficult. My legs are afraid of slipping, toppling over; they seem to belong to a man making his way across a sheet of ice. As soon as I set foot in the corridor, I begin shivering all over.

On my way to the lavatory I detect a strong odor of cabbage and some other kind of food. The very thought of food disgusts me, but my disgust is of a special variety: if I feel nauseous, it is not from a full stomach but from a mental, psychic upheaval. My throat feels so tight and sensitive that the smallest scrap of food would either lodge in it or tear it apart.

Back in the room I find a glass of water on the piano. "Take a drink," says Mik. (He, too, talks through his teeth and hides his eyes.) "It will do you good."

Although I strain to move rapidly, my arm, describing a kind of fearful trajectory, no more than inches its way towards the glass. My tongue and the roof of my mouth are hard and dry, but the water does not moisten them; it merely gives them a chill. Each swallow makes me gag. It is like taking medicine.

"The best thing is black coffee," says Mik, "but there isn't any. Have a smoke. That helps too."

I light a cigarette. Every time I bring it to my lips, I surprise them in a continuous sucking movement. I seem to be using it, the sucking movement, as a vent for unbearable, surplus euphoria. I know that if I absolutely had to I could stop it, but to do so would be as unnatural as keeping one's hands at one's sides while running.

Yet whether from the water or the cigarette or the latest dose of the now dwindling cocaine, my icy, awkward body, anxious lest it tip or turn something over, my frozen legs, feeling their way along the floor as if it were a sheet of ice, my whole morbid state—they are nothing but a pitiful cover for a quietly pulsating core of exaltation.

I walk over to the table. While I take a step, while I bend my knee and, in abject fear, place my foot back on the floor, the process seems so painfully long as never to end. But once the step is taken and the process complete, the result (to say nothing of the strenuous efforts accompanying it) appears so phantasmally instantaneous in my memory as never to have existed. And it is thus, back and forth between painfully long process and phantasmally instantaneous result, that the whole night passes.

Long, interminably long, the process of dressing, of aiming trembling arms at greatcoat sleeves, so that Mik and I, as I have proposed in a voice cracking with glee, may go back to my flat, pick up something of value there, and buy a few more packets with it. But here we are standing in the corridor with our coats on, and I do not seem to have exerted the slightest effort.

Long, interminably long, the perilous descent of the stairs, which might as well be covered with ice so carefully must I watch my step and counter the compulsion to rush forward in spurts, as if a dog is at my heels. But here we are standing in the vestibule, and I have all but forgotten the terrible torture of the stairs; the stairs have vanished, and we seem to have entered the street directly from the room.

Long, interminably long, the drive through the deserted city, shrill with frost, and the back-breaking chill, the rags of steam, the golden thread of streetlamps waving wetly in tearing eyes and disappearing when I blink. But here we are, standing by the gate, and none of it seems to have existed; again, we seem to have come directly from Hirghe's room.

Long, interminably long, the trembling in the cold at the shining green moon of a door until a burst of yellow with Matvei in the middle appears behind it, the ascent of the stairs and unlocking of the flat, the groping through black hall and dining room into Mother's silent bedchamber, and the sweet shudder of love for her, a love I have never known before, never experienced, and a feeling of joy and adoration as though the only reason I am slipping into her room is to do her some good, kind, beneficial deed. It seems to take forever before I make my way over to her mirror-faced wardrobe, which I pull open with a jerk (if I humored it along slowly and cautiously it would only creak the more), sending the reflection of my mother's sleeping head up toward the night light, then rocking it back and forth. The whole process seems long, painful, interminable at first and then so phantasmal as never to have existed: searching the drawer of cheap, caramel-smelling linen, finding the brooch, returning along the stairs, slipping past a Matvei determined to look into my terrible eyes, trekking arduously across the snow-covered yard (not until I reach the sleigh do I realize I am still on tiptoe), climbing into the sleigh atremble with the fear that it will jerk forward and throw me from the seat, and arriving back in the overheated silence of Hirghe's room.

The back of my neck feels tight, shackled. I strain my eyes as I might if I were moving quickly through a dark room, afraid of running into a sharp object, but neither my constant blinking nor the clear visibility of everything around me brings relief. I close my eyes, but the tension merely passes to my eyelids, which ache as if expecting a blow.

I am standing at the table. The longer I stand, the stiffer I grow and the harder I find it to move. All through the night my body has either stiffened into inertia and nailed me to the spot or hurtled me into action impossible to control. Down in the street with Mik the first few steps were terribly difficult; then everything inside me began twitching, my legs started working as if by electricity, and a dull irritation pulsed ever so insanely inside me whenever a passerby appeared in sight: I could not pass him for fear of knocking him over or bumping into the building next to him and knocking myself over, yet I found it utterly beyond my will to slow my stride.

Now Mik comes back into the room carrying some new packets of cocaine. He closes the door with the strangest of gestures, apparently afraid it will collapse on him. The overhead light is off, the room nearly dark. Nelly and Zander stand pressed together between a large cabinet and a set of double curtains in the fluttering, autumnal light of the candle. Their heads strain upwards, listening for something, as it were. Because of the curvature in Nelly's neck her head veers off to one side, the side the nocturnal noises whispering menacingly through the flat seem to be coming from. Their eyes are insanely still. Everything in the room has stopped but their lips.

"Tsst, tsst, tsst," Nelly sputters in a quick succession of sibilants.

"Somebody's coming," Zander whispers. "Somebody's coming!" he repeats in a shouted whisper, his head shaking all the while.

I, too, am contaminated; I, too, have caught their fears. I, too, can think of nothing more terrifying than a spry and bustling daylight person bursting in on our dark and silent room and seeing us all in the state we are in, seeing our eyes. I, too, have the impression it would take only a single shot or piercing cry or wild bark to snap the thread that dangles my dully pounding brain. My head is stretched so tight that the chair I am sitting in seems to be rocking. My body is cold, frozen stiff, disconnected from my head. To feel my arms or legs I have to move them.

There are people all around me. Many, many

people. It is no hallucination: I see them inside not outside myself. I see students—male and female—and non-students as well, but they all have something unusual about them: they are all misshapen, cross-eyed, noseless, long-haired, bearded . . .

"Oh, Professor Maslennikov," one of the young women cries out in ecstasy, stretching out her arms to me from a distance, "Professor Maslennikov, would you lecture on sports today?" She has only one eye.

The misshapen, cross-eyed, bearded, and long-haired—people so deformed they cannot, are afraid to take their coats off—all shriek, "Yes, Professor Maslennikov! Sports! Sports! Give us a definition of athletics!"

I flash a casual smile, and the misshapen, cross-eyed, bearded, and long-haired all fall silent. "Athletics, ladies and gentlemen, is the expenditure of physical energy under conditions of mutual competition and total lack of productivity."

The armless, misshapen, and cross-eyed scream, "More! More! Go on!", and the scholarly young woman with one eye elbows her way through the crowd towards the podium saying "Excuse me, dear colleague" each time she pokes someone in the face. I raise my hand. Silence.

"The important thing for us, ladies and gentlemen," I whisper, "is not so much athletics itself, its essence, as the impact it has on society and even, if I may be so bold, on the state. Permit me, therefore, to begin my talk with several remarks about athletes rather than athletics. Oh, do not think I have in mind only the professional athlete, the kind who accepts money for competing, makes a living by competing. Not in the least. For what a man lives *by* is not nearly so important as what he lives *for*. That is why when I speak of athletes I mean all, yes, all athletes we know, irrespective of whether they consider sport a vocation or an avocation, a way of earning a living or a way of life. Anyone who has followed the growth in popularity they have enjoyed recently can tell more than mere success stories, for today's athletes are *worshiped,* and worshiped by ever broadening circles of society. Newspapers feature them, magazines publish their pictures (though what have their faces to do with it?); they are well on their way to becoming national heroes. It is one thing for a nation to be proud of its Beethovens, Voltaires, Tolstoys (though what has the nation to do with it?), but it is something else again when a nation is proud of Ivan Tsybulkin having stronger thighs than Hans Müller. Do you not agree, ladies and gentlemen, that pride of that ilk testifies less to Tsybulkin's strength and vigor than to the nation's infirmity, morbidity? For when the public applauds Ivan Tsybulkin, worships him in so suspect a manner, it is openly and enthusiastically declaring a willingness to exchange places, exchange lives with the object of its applause, and the greater the applause, the closer it takes us to a new stage in public opinion, and thereby in the nation as a whole, a stage in which Ivan Tsybulkin will become the highest ideal, Ivan Tsybulkin, whose only merit is a pair of good, strong thighs."

I keep whispering these words to myself, whispering them over and over. I want so much to preserve this night. I feel so good, so clear inside, and I am so utterly enraptured by this life that I want to slow it down and worship it, every second of it, yet nothing can stop it as it swiftly and irresistibly retreats.

I spy the dawn through the slit in the curtain. I feel a weighty void beneath my eyes and in my cheekbones. Everything around me is grinding to a halt. My nose, still greedily flared, is a miserable void down into the throat, and each breath I take makes a painful scratch: either the air is too coarse or the inside of my nose has grown terribly sensitive. I try to dispel the ever-growing burden of despair bearing down on me; I try to call back my thoughts, my ecstasies, the ecstasies of my bearded audience, but what comes up from my memory is the night as a whole, and I am so embarrassed, so ashamed, that for the first time in my life I truly feel I have no desire to go on living.

I begin looking for the packet of cocaine on the card table. The cards are still spread out over the table, backs up, and I carefully move them apart, first turning them over one by one, then tossing them every which way, and finally tearing them up senselessly. The awful despair I feel at not finding any cocaine grows steadily in intensity. But of course there is none to find. Mik and Zander have taken it all off for themselves.

The room is empty. Instead of going back to my chair, I collapse on the couch. Doubled over, I have terrible trouble breathing, so I try to inhale while making myself sit up, and exhale while letting myself fall back, as if the piercing column of air were capable of damping the flames of my despair. And only a clever little devil in the inner reaches of my mind, the kind who goes on shining through the most violent of my emotional hurricanes, only that little devil keeps telling me I must give in and stop thinking of cocaine, that by thinking about it—and especially about the possibility of finding some here in Hirghe's room—I am only exacerbating an already agonizing frustration.

I close my eyes in a state of misery, the horror of which I have never known before, and slowly, smoothly, the room begins to spin. But then it sags in one corner, sags deeper and deeper until it slips under me, then climbs up in back of me, then peeps out above me, and once more, but swiftly this time, sags and falls.

I open my eyes. The room has returned to its place, though my head keeps spinning and, since my neck refuses to support it, collapses on my chest. The room turns upside down again.

"What have they done?" I whisper. "What have they done to me?" And after a meaningless pause: "I suppose I'm ruined."

But that same little devil—the clever one who (if I listen to him, that is) poisons the most blissful of feelings with doubt and soothes the basest despair with hope, who believes in nothing whatever—that little devil responds as follows: "Everything you say—it's all an act. You're not ruined, and if you're feeling rotten, well then, put on your coat and go out and get some fresh air. It won't do you any good to sit there and mope."

5

It was still quite dark outside; the sullied raspberry sky hung low. A tram jangled past, its bulbs shining like flat oranges through the snow-covered windows. I imagined the crackling frost inside the tram, the sour-smelling wet cloth, the people packed tightly together shrouding one another in the dense vapors of morning's putrid breath.

A man with a cane was walking ahead of me. Every few steps he would stop, lean his stomach on the cane, clear his throat long and loud, and spew out the contents. Whenever he stopped and coughed, his eyes would look down at the snow as though they saw something horrible in it. And each time he brought up his green sputum, I could not help gulping and imagining I was swallowing it. It had never occurred to me that people, any people, could inspire the unbounded disgust I experienced that morning.

At the next corner, where the wind was battering some theater bills glued to a pillar, I saw a little girl run into the street in front of a van with clanking chains. Her mother stood petrified on the other side of the street until the girl ran up to her, unscathed. Then she grabbed her by the arm and gave her a spanking. The child howled with pain, her eyes mere slits, her mouth a perfect square. It was only too obvious: fear or no fear, mother was taking revenge on child. And if motherhood is the pride of humanity, what must the rest of us be like?

It was light by then and morning by the time I entered our courtyard. The path had been freshly sprinkled with bright yellow sand, though it already bore the pockmarked traces of a new pair of galoshes. The Masters' Garden looked unkempt and abandoned: the snow piled up in it from all over the yard had raised its level and dwarfed the trees, and the wet, black boards buried randomly in the drifts were barely recognizable as summer's benches.

Matvei was cleaning the door handle with whiting, his free hand following the same pattern as the hand that was doing the work, but the phone rang as I came up to him, and he was obliged to run off to the booth. I climbed the stairs and unlocked the door. Then I tossed my cap on the base of the hanging mirror, which rocked the dining room table and the samovar left on it the evening before, and, trying to make as little noise as possible, tiptoed down the passageway and into my room.

My first impression was one of surprise at finding the lamp on; I even tried to recall when I could have forgotten to turn it off. And then what did I see rising painfully out of the armchair but the figure of my mother. Looking me straight in the eye, she began moving slowly towards me. The moment her glance met mine, everything around me became terribly quiet. The water in the kitchen dripped like snapping strings.

"Thief," said my mother, barely moving her lips. She said it, that awful word, in a clear whisper; nor did she move a bone in her small yellow face when, yielding to some inner necessity which simultaneously compelled and appalled me, I swung my arm and struck her in the face.

"My son is a thief," she whispered calmly and sorrowfully, as if thinking out loud, and with a terrible shake of the head she slowed her step even more, expecting, perhaps, a new blow. Then she turned in the direction of the door, her shoulders and arms drooping pitiably.

From the radiator under the stone windowsill came a sudden succession of clicking, hissing, and gurgling sounds and a burst of oppressive heat. The yellow filament of the lamp continued glowing dully. My nose was so swollen I had trouble breathing. Through the window I could see the neighboring house start to wrinkle and its chimney veer off, wet and shiny, into the metallic skies. But I did not think to wipe my tear-filled eyes.

6

Half an hour later I was standing in front of Yag's house. There I found a cab laden with suitcases and Yag himself in traveling clothes fussing with his "Spanish beauty." The moment he saw me he ran up to me—as fast as his enormous fur coat would allow—and threw his arms around me. I told him briefly that I had had trouble at home and was more or less without a roof over my head . . . and he, in the elated spirit of one about to take off on a trip, did not even let me finish. How wonderful it was, he shouted, a true godsend: he had been looking for somebody to live in his place while he was gone.

And so saying, he grabbed me by the arm and dragged me into the house, telling a maid carrying out a valise, as we ran past without stopping, that I would be staying in his room for the three months he was away in Kazan, and—still running—pulled me up the stairs and through the large room (the one with the piano and chandelier) to his door, put the key in the lock, and with a gruff look on his face stuffed a packet of banknotes into my hand, shaking his head as if to say "No arguments," whereupon, giving me another quick hug and apologizing for rushing so (he was afraid of missing his train), he waved good-bye and was off.

Alone, I unlocked the door and entered my new lodgings with strange misgivings. Everything had happened too quickly, and the sleepless night had left me feeling distinctly queasy. The room was a mess; it had the forlorn, forsaken aura of departure about it. On the table I found a few slices of bread and two plates smeared with the leftovers of the previous evening meal. I broke off a piece of the bread, but the moment it entered my mouth, I felt an unprecedented void and twitching airiness in the area of my cheekbones, and I swallowed the bread whole, without a chew: I was experiencing post-cocaine hunger for the first time. I set to eating voraciously, tearing the greasy meat apart with my fingers. With hands and neck trembling, on the brink of stupor, I stuffed my mouth, swallowed, stuffed it again. I felt like roaring—and like laughing a nervous little laugh at feeling like roaring. And when, having eaten everything there was to eat and feeling heavy with sleep (though I could have devoured a good deal more), I made my way over to the couch and lay down, I immediately noted a rather pleasant throbbing sensation in my legs. And I dreamed of my poor, old mother in her tattered coat trudging through the city straining her dim, horror-stricken eyes in search of me.

REFLECTIONS

1

Next morning, after a good night's sleep, I went back to Hirghe's and purchased a gram and a half of cocaine from him. And so it continued, day after day.

Even as I write, I cannot help picturing a disdainful smile on the face of whoever happens to come by these sad notes. And I can well understand that normal human beings are likely to interpret the words I use to convey the power of cocaine as a portrait of my own weakness. I also realize that such an interpretation is bound to provoke a feeling of alienation in them, a feeling so contemptuous and disdainful that it will alienate even the most sympathetic of readers once they decide that the concatenation of circumstances leading to the narrator's ruin could in no wise (should something similar befall them) ruin or even alter *their* lives.

The reason I bring all this up is that I too would have felt disdainful and alienated without that first night of cocaine, and only now, on the road to destruction, do I see that *my* disdain would have resulted not so much from self-glorification as from an underestimation of the power the drug wields. And so, the power of cocaine. How does it make itself felt?

2

During the long nights and long days I spent under the influence of cocaine in Yag's room I came to see that what counts in life is not the events that surround one but the reflection of those events in one's consciousness. Events may change, but insofar as the changes are not reflected in one's consciousness their result is nil. Thus, for example, a man basking in the aura of his riches will continue to feel himself a millionaire so long as he is unaware that the bank where he keeps his capital has gone under; a man basking in the aura of his offspring will continue to feel himself a father until he learns that his child has been run over. Man lives not by the events surrounding him, therefore, but by the reflection of those events in his consciousness.

All of a man's life—his work, his deeds, his will, his physical and mental prowess—is completely and utterly devoted to, fixed on bringing about one or another event in the external world, though not so much to experience the event in itself as to experience the reflection of the event on his consciousness. And if, to take it all a step further, everything a man does he does to bring about only those events which, when reflected in his consciousness, will make him feel happiness and joy, then what he spontaneously reveals thereby is nothing less than the basic mechanism behind his life and the life of every man, evil and cruel or good and kind.

One man does everything in his power to overthrow the tsar, another to overthrow the revolutionary junta; one man wishes to strike it rich, another gives his fortune to the poor. Yet what do these contrasts show but the diversity of human activity, which serves at best (and not in every case) as a kind of individual personality index. The *reason* behind human activity, as diverse as that activity may be, is always one: man's need to bring about events in the external world which, when reflected in his consciousness, will make him feel happiness.

So it was in my insignificant life as well. The road to the external event was well marked: I wished to become a rich and famous lawyer. It would seem I had only to take the road and follow it to the end, especially since I had much to recommend me (or so I tried to convince myself). But oddly enough, the more time I spent making my way towards the cherished goal, the more often I would stretch out on the couch in my dark room and imagine I was what I intended to become, my penchant for sloth and reverie persuading me that there was no point in laying out so great an expenditure of time and energy to bring the external events to fruition when my happiness would be all the stronger if the events leading up to it came about rapidly and unexpectedly.

But such was the force of habit that even in my dreams of happiness I thought chiefly of the event rather than the feeling of happiness, certain that the event (should it but occur) would lead to the happiness I desired. I was incapable of divorcing the two.

The problem was that before I first came in contact with cocaine I assumed that happiness was an entity, while in fact all human happiness consists of a clever fusion of two elements: 1) the physical feeling of happiness, and 2) the external event providing the psychic impetus for that feeling. Not until I first tried cocaine did I see the light; not until then did I see that the external event I had dreamed of bringing about—the result I had been slaving day and night for and yet might never manage to achieve—the external event was essential only insofar as I needed its reflection to make me feel happy. What if, as I was convinced, a tiny speck of cocaine could provide my organism with instantaneous happiness on a scale I had never dreamed of before? Then the need for any event whatever disappeared and, with it, the need for expending great amounts of work, time, and energy to bring it about.

Therein lay the power of cocaine—in its ability to produce a feeling of physical happiness psychically independent of all external events, even when the reflection of the events in my consciousness would otherwise have produced feelings of grief, depression, and despair. And it was that property of the drug that exerted so terribly strong an attraction on me that I neither could nor would oppose or resist it. The only way

I could have done so was if the feeling of happiness had come less from bringing about the external event than from the work, the effort, the energy invested in bringing it about. But that was a kind of happiness I had never known.

3

Of course, everything I have said thus far about cocaine must be understood only as the opinion of someone who has only just begun to take the drug and not as a general statement. The neophyte does indeed believe that the main property of cocaine is its ability to make him feel happy, much as the mouse, before it is caught, believes that the main property of mousetraps is to provide him with lard.

The most awful aftereffect of cocaine, and one that followed the hours of euphoria without fail, was the agonizing reaction which doctors call depression and which took hold of me the instant I finished the last grain of powder. It would go on for what seemed an eternity—though by the clock it was only three or four hours—and consisted of the deepest, darkest misery imaginable. True, my mind knew that it would be over in a few hours, but my body could not believe it.

It is a well-known fact that the more a person is ruled by his emotions the less capable he is of lucid observation. The feelings I experienced under the spell of cocaine were so potent that my power of self-observation dwindled to a state found only in certain of mental illnesses; my "feeling I" grew to such proportions that my "self-observing I" all but ceased operation. There being nothing left to bridle my feelings, they poured out with total abandon—in my face, in my movements, in everything I did. But the moment the cocaine was gone and the misery took over, I began to see myself for what I was; indeed, the misery consisted largely in seeing myself as I had been while under the influence of the drug.

Slumped over as if nauseous, the nails of one hand digging into the palm of the other, I recalled every sinister, shameful detail. Standing frozen by the door of Yag's silent room at night, trembling with the idiotic but insuperable fear that someone was creeping along the passageway about to burst in on me and peer into my frightful eyes. And stealing slowly, ever so slowly, up to the dark, blindless window, certain that the moment I turned my back someone would glower at me through it, yet perfectly aware it was on the second floor. And turning off the lamp and its almost audible glare, which seemed to invite intruders. And lying on the couch, straining my neck to keep my head from touching the pillow and waking the entire house with the racket. And staring into the vibrating red darkness, my eyes aching with terror at the imminent prospect of being gouged. And striking match after match, my hand so numb with cold and horror that the effort appeared doomed until, after a long hiss, one would indeed take fire, and my body recoiled as the match dropped to the couch. And pulling myself up every ten minutes for a new fix, feeling for the packet, scraping the cocaine with the dull end of a steel pen-point, though even when quivering directly beneath my nostril (lifted there in the dark by a hand growing scrawnier with every night) the pen-point failed to give me my sniff: still wet from the last time round, it had moistened the cocaine, which then hardened, and all that came through was an acrid smell of rust. And answering countless calls of the bladder, forcing myself each time to overcome the panic-stricken immobility of my body and use the chamber pot there in the room, gritting my chattering teeth as I listened to the monstrous sound I made for all the building to hear, and then, sticky from a particularly pungent, fetid sweat, climbing back on the frozen mountain of a couch and falling into a state of stupefaction until the next urgent call roused me. And watching day break and objects take on shapes again, a process that did not in the least relax the muscles, which, longing for the protective covering of night and shunning the light that exposes face and eyes, contracted even more. And licking off the rusty pen-point by the morning light, delighting in the dry rush of a fresh fix from a new packet—the slight dizzy spell, the nausea-cum-bliss—then grieving at the first sounds of people in other flats awakening. And, finally, the knock at the door, returning at long, rhythmic intervals, a cough, which, though it racked the body, was necessary to dislodge the tongue, and then my voice quaking with happiness (despite the anguish) as I muttered through my teeth, "Who's there? What do you want? Who's there?" and suddenly another knock, insistent, implacable, but from a new direction: it was the sound of wood being chopped in the courtyard.

Each time I came to the end of a session I would have visions, fanciful reconstructions of what I had just been through, how I had looked and behaved, and with the visions grew the certainty that soon, very soon—if not tomorrow then next week, if not next week then next month or year—I would end up in an insane asylum. And yet I kept increasing the dose, taking as many as three and a half grams and prolonging the effect for periods of over twenty-four hours. On the one hand, I had an insatiable desire for the drug; on the other, I merely desired to postpone its ever more ominous aftereffects.

Whether because I had increased the dosage or because any poison gives the organism a rude shock—and perhaps for both reasons—the shell my cocaine bliss presented to the world eventually began to crumble. I was possessed by the strangest of manias within an hour of the first sniff. Sometimes I would run out of matches and start searching for another box, moving the furniture away from the walls, emptying out all the drawers, carrying on with great pleasure for hours at a stretch, yet knowing all the while there was not a match in the room; at other times I would be obsessed with some dire apprehension, yet have no idea what or whom I so dreaded, and crouch in abject fear, crouch—again, for hours—by the door, torn between the unbearable need for a new fix, which meant going back to the couch, and the terrible risk involved in leaving the door unguarded for even a moment; at yet other times—and these had begun to grow in frequency lately—I would be set upon by all my manias at once, and then my nerves would be strained to the breaking point.

One night, while everyone was asleep and I had

my ear to the door keeping vigil, I heard a sudden resonant noise—the sort of bang one sometimes hears in the night—followed immediately by a long wail. It was a moment or two before I realized that it was I who had wailed and *my* hand that was clamped over my mouth.

4

One fearful question hung over me throughout my cocaine period. I say "fearful" because while one answer merely led up a blind alley, the other led to the most terrifying of world views, an affront to what is purest and most tender in man and what even the lowest of the low hold in awe: the human soul.

It all began, as such things often do, with something trifling. For what is so extraordinary about the fact that as long as cocaine is effective its devotees feel the most noble and humane of sentiments (extreme cordiality, generosity, and so on) and the moment it loses its power they are possessed by the basest, most bestial of sentiments (rage, animosity, cruelty)? Nothing at all.

And yet, the fateful question arose as a result of this succession of sentiments.

It was simple enough to ascribe my good, humane feelings to the drug's narcotic influence, but how to account for the others? How to explain the inevitability with which, after cocaine, I fell prey to evil feelings? How to explain the absolute and constant recurrence of a phenomenon that could not but lead me to believe that my most humane sentiments were inextricably bound to my most bestial sentiments and that once I began straining the limits of one set of feelings I would necessarily call forth the other. It was an hourglass situation: as one vessel emptied, the other necessarily filled.

Hence the question: Did this succession of sentiments constitute nothing more than a by-product of cocaine, one it imposed upon my organism; or was it a property peculiar to my organism, one the cocaine only brought out more clearly?

A positive answer to the first part would have led nowhere; a positive answer to the second part opened up a number of possibilities. For by attributing so extreme a reaction to my feelings (which the cocaine simply reinforced), I was clearly constrained to recognize that, even without cocaine, any upsurge in humane sentiment on my part would, by way of reaction, give rise to bursts of bestiality.

So I asked myself, "Isn't the human soul somewhat like a swing which, once given a push in the direction of humanity, is ipso facto predisposed to return in the direction of bestiality?" I tried to come up with a simple, everyday example to confirm my supposition, and I think I found one.

Say a good, kind, impressionable youth named Ivanov is at the theater. It is the third act of a sentimental play. The villains seem about to triumph, though of course they are on the brink of disaster; the heroes are on the brink of disaster, so of course a happy end is nigh. Indeed, everything is moving in the direction of the fairest and happiest of endings, the kind to which Ivanov's noble soul aspires.

Under the exhilarating influence of the theater, of the love he feels for the personifications of honor, virtue, and suffering he sees on the stage and whose happiness means so much to him, the crystalline quiver of the noblest and most humane sentiments grows stronger and stronger within him. Not a tinge of pettiness or lust or rage does he feel or could he possibly feel at such a moment—not our good, kind Ivanov. There he sits, in the inviolate darkness and silence of the theater, his face fairly burning, his soul sweetly longing to make an immediate sacrifice in the name of the highest of human ideals.

Then suddenly, out of the darkness, out of a silence saturated with human emotion, comes a loud, rasping, dog-like cough. It is Ivanov's neighbor. As the noise assaults his ears, Ivanov feels something frightful, terrifying, something bestial rising up within him, taking over. "*Damn* you and your cough!" he spits out at last in a venomous whisper. By this time he is completely drunk with hate, and though he keeps his eyes on the stage, his fury at the coughing neighbor is such that he is incapable of understanding a word. Try as he might, he is unable to regain his composure; he cannot help thinking that only a moment earlier he had only one desire: to strike his neighbor, to annihilate him, and put an end to his exasperating cough.

"What causes so sudden and diabolical an outburst in a youth like Ivanov?" I asked myself. There can be only one answer: the overexcitation of his highest and most noble sentiments. But could it not perhaps be due entirely to the cough? Alas, it could not. If his neighbor had burst out coughing in a tram (or anywhere where Ivanov was in a less heightened state), he would never have provoked such rage in so benign a youth. Thus, the coughing was no more than an excuse to liberate a preexistent feeling to which his spiritual constitution had predisposed him.

And what exactly is his spiritual constitution? Supposing we were wrong to ascribe noble, humane sentiments to him. Let us then ignore them for the moment and try to compile a list of all the other feelings a man at the theater is likely to experience. In fact, the list is not long. Nuances aside, it consists of only two items: Ivanov was either 1) in a malicious mood, or 2) bored and indifferent.

If, however, Ivanov had been in a malicious mood even before his neighbor started coughing, if he had been furious with the actors for their poor performance or with the playwright for the immorality of his work or with himself for having squandered his last kopeck on the evening, would he have experienced so wild and bestial a fit of hate towards the man? Hardly. In the worst case he would have been vaguely annoyed and grumbled something like "And now you and your cough." What is that to the desire to strike and destroy a man! Thus, the hypothesis that Ivanov was in a malicious mood before the incident and that it was his mood which provoked the outburst—this hypothesis must be rejected.

Let us assume, to continue, that Ivanov was suffering from boredom and indifference. Perhaps *these* were the feelings that led him to explode. But no, that is impossible. For if his mood was one of cold indifference, if watching the stage only made him bored, then how could he have felt the slightest desire to lash out at a coughing neighbor? Not only would he have felt no desire to hurt him, he might well have pitied the poor fellow.

And so we must perforce return to our original hypothesis, namely that the most noble and human sentiments lie at the base of the bestial irritation that welled up in him at the theater. Of course, even the most credulous among us may balk at this example. Have we the right to spout generalities about the human soul on the sole basis of Ivanov's rage when close to a thousand people with the noblest of sentiments experienced the same dramatic tension without feeling a diabolical desire to strike anyone, without marching out of the theater in a rage?

Let us, then, examine the problem from another angle. Even though the rest of the audience shows no sign of bestiality, we cannot necessarily conclude it has none. What if its animal instinct failed to show because it had been *satisfied,* satisfied in precisely the same manner as Ivanov's would have been had he struck his neighbor and met with no resistance.

No play can succeed in evoking noble sentiments unless its characters, despite the trials they must endure, are imbued with humility, tender hearts, and a deep sense of honor—or at least such is the view of the more spiritually sensitive members of the audience. But since, of course, a play must have villains as well as angels, ought we not ask whether the cruel and bloody comeuppance visited upon those villains in the name of virtue at the end of every performance does not assuage the animal instincts in us; in other words, once they have been tamed and satisfied, we, too, may leave the theater tame and satisfied. Who of us will not admit to a rush of pleasure when the hero plants his dagger firmly in the heart of the villain? "Granted," you may reply, "but that is a feeling of justice." Quite so, a feeling of justice. The uplifting, the divine feeling of justice. And where does it lead, pray tell? To pleasure in murder and bestiality. "But against villainy," you object. To which we respond that it does not matter; what matters is that the pleasure we feel at the sight of human blood can spring only from a base of bloodthirsty malice and hate. And even if these vile, these repugnant feelings spring in turn from the love which a poor, unfortunate hero has inspired in us and which offers our bestiality a quiet, clandestine escape from the sense of nobility the play has revived in us, do they not, for all that, point directly to the fearsome, murky nature of our souls?

For all we should have to do is fill our theaters with plays in which villains not only survive, not only escape punishment, but triumph, plays in which villains triumph and the virtuous poor succumb, and we should soon see people pouring into the streets in revolt, rebellion, insurrection. But, you may object again, it would be a revolt in the name of justice, in the name of the most noble of human feelings. And you are of course correct, perfectly correct. But have a look at us as we come out to revolt in the name of humanity, have a good look at our faces, our lips, and especially our eyes, and if you refuse to see that you are surrounded by wild animals then you had best beat a hasty retreat: your inability to distinguish man from beast may cost you your life.

And why is it—since only plays in which vice reigns triumphant and virtue expires are true-to-life—why is it that in life we accept the triumph of vice with the greatest equanimity while in the theater we rant and rave against it like beasts? Is it not curious that one and the same image can leave a man calm and collected in one instance (life) and arouse his ire and indignation in another (the theater)? And is this not clear proof that the cause of the feelings with which we react to external events lies not in the character of those events but in the state of our souls? So basic a question requires a response of the utmost precision.

The response is, clearly, that in life we are cowardly and insincere and primarily concerned with our personal well-being, and so in life we flatter and abet (and sometimes even personify) the very villains who so incense and infuriate us in the theater; in the theater we have the personal quest for earthly pleasures cleansed from our souls—indeed, there is nothing the slightest bit personal to sully the nobility of our sentiments—and so in the theater we are free to be purer and to allow our finest, most humane feelings and aspirations to guide us.

If all this is so, however, we are faced with a new and equally frightful thought, namely, that if in life we fail to seethe and rebel and turn into beasts, if we fail to kill one another in the name of justice, it is only because we are low, base, self-seeking—in a word, evil. For if in life, as in the theater, we gave vent to our better instincts, imbued by feelings of love for the weak and downtrodden, we should commit or desire to commit (which, inasmuch as we are speaking in spiritual terms, amounts to the same) a quantity of villainies, of bloody, torturous acts and vengeful murders that no blackguard has ever perpetrated or dreamed of perpetrating for personal profit or gain.

At times I even feel moved to address all future prophets of mankind as follows: "Prophets! Dear, kind prophets! Leave us alone. Do not try to fan the flames of lofty sentiments in our souls; do not try to make us better than we are. For so long as we are bad, we limit ourselves to petty felonies; as we grow better, we kill.

"Try to understand, dear prophets, that it is neither perfidy nor cunning nor vice that forces us to rage like vengeful animals; it is our inborn feelings of humanity and justice: without nobility of the soul we should never know righteous indignation. And try to understand that our souls work like swings: the stronger the push up towards the nobility of the soul, the stronger the swoop down towards the fury of the beast.

"The push we tend to give our spiritual swings—the push up toward humanity—and the swoop down towards bestiality that inevitably ensues have left a bloody trail through the history of mankind, and the more passionately an age pushes in the direction of the spirit, the more terrible are the cruelties and satanic transgressions committed in its name.

"Like a bear which, when it butts a log on a rope with its bleeding head, receives more and more stunning blows the harder it butts, man suffers from the ups and downs of his soul. But no matter how he tires of them and no matter how he tries to escape—whether he goes on butting until a particularly strong blow splits his head open or whether he wills the spiritual swing to a halt and lives out the rest of his days without feelings, in other words, outside humanity—he is doomed to consummate the curse of this strange and terrible aspect of the human soul."

Such were the thoughts that would invade me whenever silence descended on the house and night on the courtyard and the green lamp [illegible]ed its light on the desk; they had the same destructive influence on my will to live as the white poison flickering through my head had on my organism.

5

I am in a boyar hall with impressive high-backed chairs, low vaulted ceilings, and a feeling of heavy gloom. The guests, all formally dressed, are taking their places round a table spread with red velvet. The centerpiece is a swan on a golden plate. Sonya comes and sits next to me, and I know I am at our wedding. Even though the woman at my side does not resemble Sonya in the slightest, I know she is Sonya. The guests are all seated, and I am still uncertain about how to cut and serve the swan, which is unplucked, when all of a sudden Mother enters the hall. She is wearing a tattered dress and slippers. Her tiny yellow face and white hair tremble as she peers about with cloudy, insomniac eyes, but they clear and sparkle, bright and terrible, the moment they light on me. I signal to her to stay away—it is awkward for me to acknowledge her here—and she understands. Smiling piteously, she wedges her shriveled little body in sideways at the table. Meanwhile, some servants in red livery and white gloves take away the swan, while others lay the table and circulate with platters of food. One of them bends over to serve my mother, and, noticing how she is dressed, is about to move on, but she has picked up the serving spoon and begins filling her plate. I am mortified. What if people happen to look in her direction? While Mother continues piling food on her plate, the servant makes a face that alarms me even more, and after she has accumulated a huge mound he arrogantly removes the platter and marches off. When Mother turns to put the spoon back and sees that the servant is gone, she begins eating with it. Suddenly she undergoes a sordid change. She begins gulping down the food, quickly, voraciously, her chin pumping away, her eyes darting from one place to the next, the wrinkles in her forehead filling with sweat. And as she stuffs the food into her mouth, she mutters maliciously, "Oh, how I wike it! How I wike it!" I begin to look at her in a new way. All at once I realize that she too is flesh and blood. All at once I realize that the love she bears me represents only a fraction of her feelings, that in addition to that love she, like every other human being, has intestines, arteries, blood, and sexual organs, and that she cannot help loving her physical body more than she loves me. And all at once I am overcome by a feeling of such misery and isolation that I feel like moaning. By this time she has finished everything on her plate and begun squirming on her chair. The people sitting near her can tell immediately that her stomach is upset and that she badly needs to leave the room. The servant—smiling to show that it is beneath his dignity to take so pitiful an old woman seriously, yet not laughing, which is beneath his dignity in general—offers to escort her to the door. She stands with great difficulty, leaning all her weight on the table. Now everyone has noticed her and begun to laugh—guests, servants, Sonya—and in an orgy of self-reproach I join them. On her way out she is forced to pass in review before them and all their laughing eyes and mouths. She must also pass before me. And now that I have laughed with them, I am as much a stranger to her as they are. And pass before them she does. Hunched and shaking, she passes before them; she even smiles, smiles a pathetic smile, as if apologizing for her poor, weak body. Once she is gone, the laughter subsides, though the servants still smile their scorn, a sign perhaps that what has happened is merely a harbinger of things to come. For suddenly I see a military guard fall in by the door, a military guard replete with rifles and bayonets. And all but hidden behind them stands my mother. She tries to make her way through to me, but the soldiers hold her back. "Vadya, my boy," she keeps repeating. "Vadya, my son." My eyes find hers, our eyes meet lovingly, they call to one another. She makes one more attempt to move forward, but a soldier leaps after her, and his bayonet sinks with remarkable ease into her stomach. "My boy, my Vadya, my son," she says calmly, holding on to the bayonet with a smile. It is a smile that tells all: that she knows it is on my orders that she has been forbidden to come to me, that she is dying, that she is not angry with me, that she understands me, understands how impossible she is to love.

And then I could stand no more. I gave myself a mighty wrench, felt a painful twist inside me, and awoke. It was night. I lay fully dressed on the couch.

The light on the desk still shone under its green cap. I sat up, lowered my legs to the floor, and suddenly I was terrified. I was terrified as only grown men and women can be when they wake in the middle of the night and begin to realize, in the absolute silence and solitude all around them, that it is not only their dream that has woken them, that it is their whole way of life. "What is happening to me in this awful house? Why am I living here? What sort of delirious thoughts have I been having here?" There I sat, shivering with cold in an unheated room that had not been tidied in weeks, my lips whispering words needing no response, because even as I said them I saw images forming in my head, images vague but terrifying, so terrifying that I felt one of my hands clutching the other.

Having sat thus for what seemed like hours, I pried my hands apart (my fingers felt as though they had been glued together) and started putting on my shoes. I had a hard time of it: my socks had rotted through in places, my feet gave off a putrid odor, and my laces were all in knots. Full of disgust at my own slovenliness, I pulled myself up, slipped on my overcoat, cap, and galoshes, turned up my collar, and was about to go over to the desk and turn off the lamp when I suddenly felt a bit faint and had to sit down. The moment I did so, however, I was overcome by a wave of exhaustion bordering on nausea. After forcing my arm to stretch out and turn off the lamp, I sat in the dark until the exhaustion left me. I was then able to leave the room and feel my way into the hall without difficulty. From there—and still in the dark—I proceeded to the front door, which I unlocked carefully and could hardly hold back, so strong was the wind from the street.

Outside, the wind swept icily along. Dry snow flurried down past yellow streetlamps from windows, fences, and rooftops in the deserted distance. Gasping for breath in the wind and hunching forward against the cold, I had scarcely reached the corner before I was frozen through.

The street opened on a square with a campfire burning in it: the wind tugged at the red hair of the flames, and sparks exploded into the smoke; the tram rails nearby glowed a rosy silver; the house across the street fairly glittered. Near the fire a peasant's sheepskin coat bobbed up and down, first hugging itself, then letting itself go.

I walked as quickly as I could. Snow poured beneath my galoshes like milk from a bucket. I turned down a long street, and the wind calmed down a bit. The moonlight divided the street into two distinct parts—one ink-black, the other emerald-green—and walking along the dark side I followed the shadow of my head as it crossed the black border and rolled into the middle of the street. The moon itself was nowhere to be seen, but when I lifted my head I could see its reflection running from upper-story window to upper-story window, flashing bright green in each one.

Thus absorbed in my thoughts and taking one or another street more or less by instinct, I suddenly found myself before the gates to the house where my mother lived. Pulling the wobbly iron ring on the wicket, I stepped into a green rectangle with my shadow in the middle and thence into the courtyard. The moon was now high in the sky behind me, and the fence lay like a dark field bordering a mere strip of yard.

Having climbed the stairs to the main entrance, I paused before the heavy door and the glitter of its brass handle. The highly polished bevels in its windows sent a thin band of light down the stairs. When at last

I gave the handle a joggle, the band of light hardly stirred: the door was locked.

Since I felt uneasy about waking Matvei, I ran down the stairs and turned into the dark, wet tunnel leading to the rubbish bins and the entrance to the back stairs. I found it strewn with birch bark and chips, for it was here the yardkeeper chopped wood, first swinging his sonorous ax, next making a bundle of logs on one of the bins, then tying them up with a pre-cut rope and flinging them over his back, and finally shuffling heavily up the stairs—the rope eating into his back and through to his rag-bound fingers, which would alternately puff up with blood or drain white—to deliver the booty to a kitchen.

Now, as I climbed the pitch-black, cat-infested stairway, holding on to the thin iron railing for dear life, I recalled the time when rubbish bins did not yet exist. I recalled the hot summer day when the courtyard suddenly resounded with a theatrical thunderclap and there, on the spot, the sheets of tin the cart had left behind were cut into proper shapes. Then, that evening, they were assembled with a great racket and an echo so clear that I actually believed the same assembly process was taking place in the neighboring yard as well. When was that? How old was I at the time?

Up I climbed the foul-smelling stairway, passing landing after landing without number, until suddenly my calves started aching strangely, as if trying to slow me down, and I turned back to the landing I had just passed, and found the door to our flat. I was about to knock—and had even prepared a facial expression to use on Nanny—when I noticed that the door was slightly ajar. "Maybe the chain is on," I thought, but no sooner did I touch it than it opened noiselessly. I was in our kitchen. Despite the dark I knew it was ours from the tick of the kitchen clock, which, like a cripple climbing stairs, had its own, irregular rhythm: two fast beats, then a rest, then one-two again.

Everything that happened in the seemingly abandoned flat that night was, from the moment I left the kitchen, quite bizarre. Thus, by the time I stopped before the door of my old room, I could not recall whether I had locked the kitchen door behind me or even whether there was a key in the lock. Nor, in the dining room, could I determine how far I had walked normally and where I had begun to slink. I could still remember that the door to my room had been locked, but why I was in a hurry to leave it, what I was horrified of—I hadn't the slightest idea.

The dining room was extremely quiet. The clock was not ticking. All I could see in the dark was that there was no cloth on the table and that the door to Mother's room was open. The door horrified me as well. I stood stock still. I did not move for so long that I felt myself totter inside. I decided to leave and return in the morning, and was about to turn and start down the passage when suddenly a distinct rustling noise came from the bedroom, and I was drawn toward it as if pulled by a string.

"Mother?" I said abruptly. "Mother?" The noise did not return; no one responded. But for some reason, after calling out to her, I felt a smile flicker across my face.

Although nothing special had occurred during that moment, I could no longer leave. Trying to make as little noise as possible, I moved forward, skirting the table and feeling my way along the backs of the chairs, until at last I reached the bedroom. The curtains were open. Slowly, stealthily I progressed to the middle of the room, but it was so dark that I instinctively turned to the window. The moonlight seemed unable to penetrate it, not even to the sill or the folds in the blinds, and the chair Mother sat in when she embroidered looked like a charred tree trunk. But when I turned away from the window, the room was darker still. Now I was almost at the bed. I could all but smell the warm odor of a body sleeping in it. I held my breath and heard my heart beating.

"Mother?" I finally called out again. "Mother?" This time my voice sounded stifled, worried, but again no one responded. And yet the very sounds I had made seemed to give me leave to draw closer and take a cautious seat at the foot of the bed. I lay my hands on the bed first to keep the springs from creaking, and felt the lace bedspread that covered the bed only by day. The bed had not been slept in; it was empty. The warm odor immediately dissipated. Still I sat down, and it was while doing so, turning my head by chance in the direction of the wardrobe, that I saw her at last. Her head was quite high, on a level with the highest arabesque on the wardrobe. My first reaction was to wonder why she had climbed so high and what she was standing on. But it immediately gave way to a repulsive weakness in my legs and bladder—the weakness of fear. Mother was not standing; she was hanging, hanging and staring at me with a gray, empty face.

"Ooh! Ooh!" I cried, running out of the room as if someone were on my tracks. "Ooh! Ooh!" I cried wildly, flying through the dining room, yet simultaneously aware I was in fact sitting at Yag's desk, trying hard to raise a head numb with sleep.

It was a late, winter dawn. I was sitting at the desk in my overcoat and galoshes with a stiff neck, stiff legs, and a throat choked with bitter tears.

6

An hour later I was bounding up the stairs, and at the sight of the familiar door my heart jumped with joy. I approached it gingerly and, not wanting to disturb anyone, rang only once. I could hear street noises through the door—a van rattling the windows as it thundered past. Downstairs the telephone gave an early morning rasp. The door did not open.

I rang again, but this time listened more carefully. There was no sign of movement in the flat; no one seemed to be living there any longer. "My God," I thought, "could something have happened? Has anything gone wrong? What will become of me then?"

Desperate, I leaned long and hard on the bell,

pressed it for all I was worth. At last I heard shuffling feet emerge from the bowels of the flat and make their way to the door. After a moment they were replaced by a key jangling in the lock. And finally the door flew open. I heaved a sigh of joy and relief. All my worries had been in vain. For standing there, alive and well, was Hirghe himself.

"So it's you," he said with indolent disgust. "And I thought there was someone here to see me. Oh well, you might as well come in."

And I went in.

EPILOGUE

Here end the notes of Vadim Maslennikov or, rather, here they break off. Maslennikov was brought, delirious, to our hospital during the terrible frosts of January 1919. Once he had regained consciousness and we could make a preliminary examination, we learned from the patient that he was a cocaine addict, that he had tried many times to break the habit, and that by dint of great effort he had succeeded in doing so for a month or two at a time. In the end, however, he always returned to it. According to his own confession, addiction had grown more painful of late, tending to irritate the psychic apparatus rather than exhilarate it. To be more explicit, if during the early stages of addiction cocaine promoted precision and acuity of consciousness, it now elicited incoherence, which, when coupled with a concomitant sense of anxiety, tended to produce hallucinations.

When the head physician asked him why he kept returning to the drug when he knew in advance that, no matter what the dosage, it would subject him to psychic torture, Maslennikov compared his state to Gogol's. Like Gogol, he said in a trembling voice, like Gogol, who, while working on the second part of *Dead Souls*, knew that the creative forces of his earlier years had dried up, that every attempt to revive them moved him further from them, yet returned day after day to the tortures of creation (for without the euphoria, the combustion of creation, life had no meaning for him)—like Gogol, he, Maslennikov, continued to succumb to his obsession even though it promised him nothing but despair.

Maslennikov exhibited all the symptoms of addiction: extensive damage to the intestinal tract, debility, chronic insomnia, apathy, cachexia, jaundice, and a number of nervous disorders, apparently of psychic origin, the precise diagnosis of which required further observation.

Clearly it made no sense to keep such a patient in a military hospital such as ours. He was informed of his imminent discharge by our chief physician, an extraordinarily kind man, who, obviously upset at not being able to help him, added that what he, Maslennikov, needed was not so much a hospital as a good psychiatric sanatorium. But gaining admission to such a sanatorium would not be easy. In our new socialist era admission depended less on illnesses presented than on services rendered to the Revolution or, failing same, the likelihood of services to be rendered in future.

Maslennikov listened morosely, a swollen eyelid giving his face a sinister cast. When asked solicitously by the head physician whether he had any relatives or friends who might be of use, have connections, he answered he had not. After a long pause he added that his mother was deceased and that his old nanny, who had made heroic sacrifices to help him through these difficult times, was herself badly in need of help. The only friends he could name were several former classmates: a certain Stein, who had recently left the country, and two others, whose whereabouts he no longer knew, namely, Yegorov and Burkewitz.

The moment he mentioned the name Burkewitz everyone present exchanged glances.

"Comrade Burkewitz?" the head physician asked. "Why, he's our direct superior. One word from him and you're saved!"

Maslennikov asked us all kinds of questions, apparently worried it was all a misunderstanding or a case of someone with the same name. He was extremely agitated and, I think, pleased when we convinced him that our Comrade Burkewitz was indeed the one he knew. The head physician informed him that the department run by Comrade Burkewitz was located in the same street as the hospital but that, since there was little chance of his finding anyone in at so late an hour, he would have to wait until the next morning to see him. He then offered Maslennikov a bed for the night, but Maslennikov declined and left the hospital.

Next morning, shortly after eleven, three errand boys from Comrade Burkewitz's department carried him in. It was too late to save him. All we could do was establish that death was due to cardiac arrest from acute cocaine poisoning and that it was unmistakably premeditated: the drug had been dissolved in water and swallowed.

The following were found in the inner breast pocket of his jacket: 1) a small calico pouch with ten silver five-kopeck pieces sewn into it, and 2) a manuscript with two words scribbled in large, jittery letters on the front page: *Burkewitz refuses.*

European Classics

M. Ageyev
Novel with Cocaine

Jerzy Andrzejewski
Ashes and Diamonds

Honoré de Balzac
The Bureaucrats

Heinrich Böll
Absent without Leave
And Never Said a Word
And Where Were You, Adam?
The Bread of Those Early Years
End of a Mission
Irish Journal
Missing Persons and Other Essays
The Safety Net
A Soldier's Legacy
The Stories of Heinrich Böll
Tomorrow and Yesterday
The Train Was on Time
What's to Become of the Boy?
Women in a River Landscape

Madeleine Bourdouxhe
La Femme de Gilles

Karel Čapek
Nine Fairy Tales
War with the Newts

Lydia Chukovskaya
Sofia Petrovna

Grazia Deledda
After the Divorce
Elias Portolu

Leonid Dobychin
The Town of N

Yury Dombrovsky
The Keeper of Antiquities

Aleksandr Druzhinin
Polinka Saks • The Story of Aleksei Dmitrich

Venedikt Erofeev
Moscow to the End of the Line

Konstantin Fedin
Cities and Years

Arne Garborg
Weary Men

Fyodor Vasilievich Gladkov
Cement

I. Grekova
The Ship of Widows

Vasily Grossman
Forever Flowing

Stefan Heym
The King David Report

Marek Hlasko
The Eighth Day of the Week

Bohumil Hrabal
Closely Watched Trains

Ilf and Petrov
The Twelve Chairs

Vsevolod Ivanov
Fertility and Other Stories

Erich Kästner
Fabian: The Story of a Moralist

Valentine Kataev
Time, Forward!

Kharms and Vvedensky
The Man with the Black Coat: Russia's Literature of the Absurd

Danilo Kiš
The Encyclopedia of the Dead
Hourglass

Ignacy Krasicki
The Adventures of Mr. Nicholas Wisdom

Miroslav Krleza
The Return of Philip Latinowicz

Curzio Malaparte
Kaputt
The Skin

Karin Michaëlis
The Dangerous Age

Neera
Teresa

V. F. Odoevsky
Russian Nights

Andrey Platonov
The Foundation Pit

Bolesław Prus
The Sins of Childhood and Other Stories

Valentin Rasputin
Farewell to Matyora

Alain Robbe-Grillet
Snapshots

Arthur Schnitzler
The Road to the Open

Yury Trifonov
Disappearance

Evgeniya Tur
Antonina

Ludvík Vaculík
The Axe

Vladimir Voinovich
The Life and Extraordinary Adventures of Private Ivan Chonkin
Pretender to the Throne

Lydia Zinovieva-Annibal
The Tragic Menagerie

Stefan Zweig
Beware of Pity